CRIMINAL JUSTICE

a novel by

Barbara J. Olexer

Joyous Publishing
Milwaukie, Oregon, USA

Cover art by Diane Andersen
Brookside Photography and Design

16-point Large Print

ISBN 978-0-9800514-2-1

Joyous Publishing
9752 SE 43rd Avenue, Unit D
Milwaukie, Oregon 97222-1717
www.joyouspub.com

Printed in the U.S.A.

by Barbara J. Olexer

NONFICTION

Presidential Education: Prelude to Power
The Enslavement of the American Indian in Colonial Times
Murder of a Soul: The Story of Captain Jack (screen biography)
What Astrology Means to You: A Handbook of Astrological Terms, Glyphs, and Applications

FICTION

They Lived Ever After
Death Takes a Flyer
Murder by Accident
If You Can't Trust Your Uncle Sam
Father to the Man
Fossil Rocks
Criminal Justice

Chapter 1

Elsa Mills stood up from her desk chair and rubbed the small of her back, stretching backwards to ease the ache.

"I'm good and sick of this baby where it is," she said. "I'll be glad when it's out where I can put it down when I get tired."

Roy Tucker in the next cubicle glanced at her, made a face of impatience, and turned his attention back to his paperwork. Elsa stuck her tongue out at the back of his head and reached to pick up her phone on the second ring.

"Elsa Mills. How may I help you?" Elsa listened a moment, then said, "Okay, I'll take it. What's the address?" She scribbled on her scratch pad, read the address and phone number back, and hung up. She took her purse out of a drawer of her desk and slung the strap over her right shoulder.

"Something?" Roy asked, hoping it wasn't going to spill over into his cubicle.

"Some scumbag father molesting his daughter. I'll take care of it."

"Maybe I'd better come along. You never know what the weirdoes will do."

"He's not with her now, she's at an aunt's. I'll pick her up and take her in."

Elsa started off but Roy called her back.

"Hey, what about paperwork?"

"I'll take her on an 'emergency, immediate danger to the child.'"

Roy shrugged and went back to his own paperwork.

Elsa signed out, left the building, and got into her little blue Honda Civic. She hated the seat belt at any time but in her eighth month of pregnancy, it was a real pain. She fastened it and pushed it under her bulging abdomen; it crossed her chest and pressed against the side of her neck but there was nothing she could do about that. Fleetingly, she wondered if it really restricted the blood flow to her brain and if so, how seriously. Well, the law was the law and as a good little (big, for the time being) bureaucrat, it behooved her to obey and let the consequences fall where they may.

It was only a little after two in the afternoon so traffic wasn't bad. She only had to swear at a little old man ahead of her at a stop light who didn't seem to know the difference between red and green, and flip the finger to a hot-shot kid – she couldn't tell if it was a boy or girl – who passed her after tail-gating her for three blocks.

The house, when she found the address, was about what she expected. Old, run-down frame house, probably a rental, with a spotty lawn. The car in the driveway was fairly new and shone brightly green in sharp contrast to the house. She snatched up her purse and a clipboard with forms clipped to it and went up the short walk to the front door.

She knocked and the door flew open. Karen Mulligan, in her early forties, so fat that she looked short and squat, stood there, a baby perched on her hip. She was well-groomed, dressed in slacks and blouse. The baby was clean, clutching a pink stuffed rabbit. Elsa was vaguely surprised at the cleanliness.

"Mrs. Mulligan?" Elsa asked.

"Yes. Are you the social worker?"

"Yes. Elsa Mills."

Elsa handed her a business card and the woman stepped back, inviting her in. She gestured at the couch. Elsa sat down on the edge of it and Mrs. Mulligan sat in a matching easy chair, holding the baby on her lap. A little boy was sitting on the floor surrounded by building blocks. But he wasn't playing with them, he was carefully watching the two women, his eyes big with uncertainty. The boy was also clean; the house was clean and neat. The places she usually went for this kind of thing weren't generally either clean or neat. Neither were the people. Still, people come all kinds and to be fair, child molestation was not exclusively a crime of the poverty stricken.

"These are my sister's kids," Karen said. "I take care of them for her while she's at work. She works at the drug store. She and her husband own it but it doesn't amount to much. I always told her that Virgil Thwait would never amount to anything but she just had to marry him. Just threw herself away and now he's done this!"

"What exactly are you accusing Mr. Thwait of, Mrs. Mulligan?"

"He's molested this sweet little baby girl. God knows how many times he's done it before and not been caught."

"How do you know she's been molested?"

"I changed her diaper a little while ago and it was bloody. Can you imagine a man doing such a thing to his own daughter?"

"Unfortunately, I don't have to imagine it, I see it all the time. I'll need the diaper for evidence. You kept it, didn't you?"

"Of course. I knew you couldn't arrest him just on my say so. It's in the bathroom, in a plastic bag."

"All right," Elsa said. "Children as young as this one can't usually tell us very much but we have to try. What's her name?"

"Logan. It's an idiotic name for a girl but my sister is a wannabe Yuppie or something. The boy's name is Griffin."

"How old is Logan?"

"About a year and a half. She was born in August and this is January. Not quite eighteen months. Griffin's four."

Elsa wrote it all down and leaned forward to Logan.

"Logan, honey," she coaxed, "that's a very nice bunny rabbit you have. May I see it?"

Logan looked a little alarmed and stuffed as much of the rabbit's front leg as possible into her mouth.

"Let me have her," Elsa instructed. Mrs. Mulligan put the baby on Elsa's lap and Elsa scooted back on the couch so she could lean back a little and make more room for her. Logan began to pucker up and looked anxiously at her aunt.

"It's okay, Logan. The nice lady just wants to talk to you."

Griffin got up and slowly edged his way around the coffee table to stand beside his aunt, his thumb in his mouth.

"Don't suck your thumb, Griffin," she ordered. She sat down and looked expectantly at Elsa.

"Logan," said Elsa softly, "did someone touch you here?" She gently patted the front of Logan's diaper.

“Daddy did,” Griffin said.

Logan smiled. “Daddy did.”

The two women exchanged significant glances.

“When, Logan? When did Daddy touch you there? Was it this day?” Elsa asked.

“Daddy did,” she said again.

“Daddy touched her there lots of times,” Griffin said. “He isn’t supposed to. It says on TV no one is supposed to touch you where your bathing suit is.”

“Did he touch her there today?” Karen asked sharply.

Griffin looked confused and scared at her tone.

“Please, Mrs. Mulligan, let me handle this. We don’t want to frighten the children more than they are already.” Elsa frowned at the other woman then smiled at the children.

“Griffin, was it today that Daddy did this to Logan?” Elsa asked softly, nodding at him encouragingly.

Griffin nodded solemnly.

“Did you see him do it?”

The boy nodded again.

“Has he done it before?”

Again the boy nodded.

Elsa motioned for Karen Mulligan to take the baby. Karen did so and sat back down, cuddling the girl protectively.

"Do your mommy and daddy fight, Griffin?" Elsa asked, taking a pen from her purse and holding the clipboard ready.

Griffin was confused. He didn't know what he was supposed to say. This strange lady was acting funny. He didn't like her.

"Answer the lady, Griffin," Karen told him.

He stuck his thumb in his mouth and blinked at his aunt.

"Griffin," Karen said impatiently. "Griffin, quit acting dumb and answer the lady. You know your mom and dad fight and argue all the time, tell the lady."

"Please, Mrs. Mulligan, let me handle this?" Elsa smiled at Griffin. "Is that right? Do Mommy and Daddy fight? Does Daddy yell at Mommy?"

Griffin nodded uncertainly and Elsa checked a box on her form. A few more questions and hesitant answers yielded more check marks.

"I've got enough for now, Mrs. Mulligan. I'll take the children and we'll be in touch. Would you get their coats and caps?"

"Wait a minute." Karen was alarmed and upset. "You're going to take the kids away? Now?"

"Of course. We can't let them go back to where they're in danger. And you have no custodial authority beyond this day-to-day babysitting arrangement, have you?"

"No, but I didn't think you'd take them away. What will I tell Rhonda when she comes to pick them up?"

"I guess you'll have to tell her about her husband. She probably already knows, they usually do. The children's coats?"

"No. No, I can't let you take them. They'll be safe here with me."

Elsa sighed. "You don't understand. Once a report of molestation has been filed, once the child is known to be in danger, we can't just leave her in that situation. They will be well taken care of."

Karen was frightened now. "I won't sign a complaint. I won't sign anything."

"Fine. It doesn't matter. You made the report to me and now it's out of your hands. The children are no longer your responsibility, they're mine. Unless you want me to take them out of here without coats, get them."

"But this is not right. Just to yank children away from their parents like this. No warning or anything."

Elsa was irritated. She struggled to her feet, knowing she looked ridiculous rising from the low seat. "Did this baby's father give her warning that she was about to be sexually molested? I can't return the child to him or leave her where she would be vulnerable to him."

"But what about Griffin? He hasn't been molested. He isn't in any danger. You don't need to take him, too."

"Mrs. Mulligan. His father is a pedophile and an abusive husband. Griffin no longer wears diapers so you have not had occasion to check. You don't really know whether he's been sexually abused, too, do you? Leave this in the hands of the professionals now. We know what we're doing."

Griffin began to cry, upset and bewildered at the argument between the stranger and his aunt. He couldn't understand what it was all about but it seemed to mean bad things were about to happen to him and Logan. He looked up at his aunt and took hold of the tail of her blouse. Logan, seeing the acrimony all around her, added her wails to Griffin's.

Karen handed Logan to Elsa, detached Griffin and swiftly went into her bedroom. She returned a moment later with the children's coats and caps. While Elsa stuck Logan's arms into her coat, Karen put Griffin into his. Caps on their heads, Elsa started to the door with Logan in one arm, leading Griffin by the hand. Karen caught up the clipboard and Elsa's handbag. Seeing the pink rabbit on the couch, she took it along. She opened the door and the cold made her catch her breath.

At the car she took Griffin's hand while Elsa

unlocked it and put Logan in the back seat in an infant carrier. Griffin renewed his bellowing and kicked and fought when Elsa attempted to put him in the back seat.

"Stop it!" Elsa ordered, shaking him by the shoulder. "Stop that!"

A lusty kick caught her on the forearm and without thinking, she slapped him on the side of the face. He screamed louder but quit fighting and allowed her to buckle him into the seat belt.

Karen leaned in to give the rabbit to Logan. The baby took it and crushed it to her, sobbing. She dropped the rabbit and held out her arms to Karen. Karen quickly closed the door and went around to the driver's side where Elsa was buckling her own seat belt. She handed the social worker her handbag and clipboard.

"Thanks," Elsa said, over the shrieks of the two children. "Wait a minute, where's my pen?"

"For God's sake," Karen cried. "Go, just go."

Chapter 2

Virgil Thwait finished counting pills from a big bottle into a little bottle, arched his back and stretched. He glanced at the watch on his wrist and the wall clock, noting that it was nearly quitting time.

Rhonda, his wife of eight years, smiled at her customer and handed her back her credit card. The woman accepted the card and her bag of cosmetics, and turned to go. Rhonda wished her a good day and, there being no other customers in the store, kicked off her high heels. She sighed gratefully and opened the till. She riffled through the bills in the cash register, estimating with fair accuracy how much was there.

"It's been a pretty good day," she said, speaking over her shoulder to her husband, as she closed the cash drawer.

"Busy, anyway. It's almost five," he added, "why don't you go on and pick up the kids? I'll close up."

"Yeah, I think I will. Pick up something for

dinner on your way home, will you?"

"All right. Chicken or Chinese?"

"How about pizza? We haven't had it for quite a while and the kids like it."

"Yeah, okay. Pizza it is."

Rhonda picked up her shoes and padded to the back of the shop in her stockings. She slipped on her flats and coat and put on her gloves.

It was cooling off outside, the sun was rapidly sliding down behind the horizon, taking its heat with it. Rhonda let her elderly white Ford sedan warm up a minute or two then dove into the rush hour traffic. It was only six miles to her sister's place but it took thirty-two minutes. She'd been tired when she left the store, she was frazzled when she got to Karen's front door. She knocked and waited impatiently for Karen to open it.

"Hi, Karen. The kids ready?"

Karen's face was ashen and she was taut with apprehension. "They're not here."

"Griffin. Logan. Come on, it's time to go."

"They're not here," Karen repeated.

Rhonda closed the door and looked at her sister uncomprehendingly.

"They're not here," Karen shouted. "Don't just stand there staring at me."

"But what do you mean?" Rhonda asked. "I don't understand. Where are they if they're not here?"

"Children's Services came and took them."

Rhonda understood the words but she couldn't seem to grasp the meaning. "Karen, you're not making sense. Why would Children's Services come and take the kids away?"

"They found out that Virgil was abusing Logan. And probably Griffin, too. They took the kids into custody for their own protection."

Rhonda stared at her sister. "What? Virgil…Logan. What?"

"Oh, come off it, Rhonda. Virgil's been sexually abusing Logan. Don't pretend you didn't know. You must have known."

"Karen. If he had, of course I would know. But he hasn't. He's not that kind of man."

"Yeah, right. Listen, either he went too far or got careless. There was blood in her diaper. Naturally, I called the child protection people and they sent a woman out to check into it. I gave her the diaper and she took the kids. I couldn't let them go back to Virgil. Obviously."

Rhonda wanted to scream obscenities at her sister. She wanted to claw the face off her. A fury so hot and violent shook her that she knew she must get out of Karen's vicinity immediately or there would be murder done.

She ran to her car, fumbled with the key in the ignition, finally got the motor started and backed down the driveway. She didn't look behind her when she got to the street and narrowly missed a red sedan as she backed one wheel over the curb and scraped it gratingly. She had no coherent thoughts as she raced to the downtown building where Children's Services was housed. In some part of her mind she knew there was no use, that the offices would be closed. But she had no where else to go to look for her children. Oh, God, her children were gone. Gone. The word pounded in her mind like a hammer beating on an anvil. Gone, gone, gone, the children are gone. The parking lot at the side of the building was nearly empty. She parked and ran to the door. It was locked. Of course it was locked, it was after five. Social workers went home at five.

Home at five. She had started home before five, going to Karen's to collect Logan and Griffin first. Virgil would be home by now and wondering where she and the kids were. She would have to go home and tell her husband what had happened to his kids. Maybe he would know what to do next. What did people do when authority took their kids away? Funny, she had never wondered that before. But it had never been her kids before, either.

She got back behind the wheel of her car and backed out of the parking slot. On the street again, she headed for home, for Virgil, for sanity and help. This couldn't be happening. Things like this happened in the slums, not to people like her. They would get the kids back and she would never see or speak to Karen again as long as she lived. She parked in the driveway of the house she and Virgil had bought when Logan was about a year old. It was a nice house with a big back yard, all fenced so the children could safely play out there. When Logan was a little older they planned to put in a swimming pool. The front was nicely landscaped with azaleas and mugho pines. Clump birch shaded the big front windows and gave the house a stylish air. Rhonda always enjoyed coming home with the knowledge that this attractive place was her home, hers to cherish and care for and bring up her children in. Tonight she saw none of it, felt nothing but the fear and shock of loss. Virgil's car, a newish, sporty little electric blue Plymouth, was there so he was home, probably wondering what was keeping her.

Rhonda ran through the front door, crying and calling for Virgil. He came out of the kitchen, caught her in his arms and held her for a moment.

"What's wrong?" he asked. "Rhonda, what's the matter? Where are the kids? The pizza's getting cold, honey."

That shocked her. Talking of cold pizza when a disaster of this magnitude had struck them. She laughed and Vigil shook her a little, holding him away from him.

“Rhonda, you are scaring the hell out of me. What’s wrong?”

“Virgil, you were right. I’m so sorry. You were right and I was wrong and I’m so sorry. You didn’t want me to leave Griffin and Logan with my sister. You didn’t trust her and you were right. I’m so sorry.”

Virgil was really alarmed by this time. He grabbed a fistful of tissues from the box on the table beside him and sat Rhonda on the sofa. He sat beside her and gave her the tissues. She dabbed at her eyes and nose.

“Stop it, Rhonda. Stop it and tell me what’s wrong and where the kids are.”

“The child welfare people came to Karen’s and took them away, Virge. I went there but the office is closed. I don’t know what to do.”

If anything, Virgil’s shock was even greater than Rhonda’s, but he was quicker to assimilate it.

“Why? Why would they do that? What did Karen tell them?”

Rhonda shook her head, hiding behind a wad of tissues.

“Rhonda. What did Karen tell them? You have to tell me. I’m sure it was a lie, whatever it was, but you have to tell me.”

“Oh, Virge, she told them that you had molested Logan. That she’d found blood in her diaper.”

Virgil instantly saw the ramifications of such an accusation. Given the social climate of the times, an accusation like that could completely wreck him. He fought down his panic.

"That bitch. That hateful, bitch. I've always known that she was a piece of shit but I didn't know she would stoop to this. God, I'd like to kill her!"

He jumped to his feet and made for the front door. Rhonda caught his arm.

"Where are you going? What are you going to do?"

"I'm going to find my kids."

"I'll go with you."

He shook her hand off his arm and went out the door. Rhonda went after him, not bothering to lock the door behind her. There was nothing of value there anymore.

Virgil hardly waited for his wife to close the car door before he backed out into the street. In front of Karen's house he slammed on the brakes and in a cold rage he went around to the back door. Rhonda followed him. All the way neither had spoken, each consumed with fear and anger.

Virgil didn't bother to knock on the back door, he simply opened it and went in. Karen was at the kitchen range, stirring something in a saucepan. She whirled around when she heard the door open and stood there looking scared when she saw

Virgil. He noted it and smiled grimly.

"Why, Karen?" he demanded. "Why did you lie about me and get my kids taken away?"

"It wasn't a lie," she insisted. "You molested that sweet baby and I put a stop to it since my sister wouldn't protect her own child."

"You know it was a lie. We gave her beets for supper last night. That's what was in her diaper. I put a note in with her clean diapers to warn you so you wouldn't think she was sick or something."

"A note?" Karen asked faintly. Then more confidently, "There was no note. And even if there was it was a lie to cover up what you've been doing."

"We did," Rhonda said in tones of great relief. "Oh, that's right, we did give her beets last night."

Karen shot her a look of triumph mingled with contempt.

"What did you do with it?" Virgil demanded. "Threw it away, of course. Where?"

He went into the living room but there was no wastebasket there. He went into the front bedroom, Karen's bedroom. There was a pink plastic wastebasket beside the dressing table. He picked it up and scrabbled through the few papers and tissues it contained. "Here it is. You read it, saw the red in the diaper, and thought you had a chance to cause trouble for me. You are a real piece of work."

Rhonda took the note from him and read it: "Karen, Logan had beets for dinner last night so don't worry if her diaper is red. Virgil."

"I didn't read it," Karen stated. "You can't prove that I ever saw it."

"Who did you call? What's the name?"

"I don't know. I don't think she said."

"Of course she gave you her name. And you're going to give it to me." Virge took a menacing step toward Karen. Karen was really frightened, looking at his face. Rhonda was looking on the countertop and table. She went into the little living room and came back with a business card.

"Here it is, Virge. Elsa Mills, Children's Services. There's no phone number but it gives the address and website URL. What did she look like, Karen?"

"I don't know. Ordinary. She just looked ordinary."

"Karen, you are my sister but I'm going to slap you silly if you don't describe this woman to me and right now."

"She was pregnant! That's all I remember."

"You fat, flabby, sorry piece of shit," Virgil said. "You've always been a first-class bitch but I had no idea you were capable of this. What's the matter with you? You just can't stand it that Rhonda and the kids and I are happy. You've always destroyed everything you touched but you aren't going to get away with this. You bitch."

"Get out of here," Karen screamed. "Get out of my house. And never come back."

Virgil folded the note carefully and put it in his wallet. He turned on his heel and left. Rhonda followed him, clutching the business card. Karen continued screaming at them as they left the house, went out to the car, and was still at it as they drove away.

Back home, Virgil parked the car but made no move to get out and go inside. Rhonda sat with him.

"What are we going to do?" she finally asked. It was the first time either of them had spoken since leaving Karen's place.

"I'll call Herb Thurman. He'll know what we ought to do."

"The lawyer? I guess so."

They sat in silence until the cold drove them into the house. Rhonda made a pot of tea and carried it into the family room where Virgil was carefully placing the note in a plastic sleeve.

"Lucky we had some of these left after you made the baby's scrapbook," he said.

Rhonda nodded but he didn't look up. She put the teapot on the desk and poured them each a cup.

"Thanks, honey," he said.

He picked up his cup and sipped, turning on

the swivel chair to face her where she sat on the old blue couch. She was crying softly.

“Don’t cry, Rhonda. It’s going to be all right.”

“I can’t help it. I don’t know where my babies are. They must be scared and lonesome. Who’s going to give them their baths and tell them bedtime stories? They’ll need jammies and clean clothes for tomorrow. No one will know that Griffin doesn’t like eggs for breakfast or that Logan is allergic to orange juice. Who is taking care of them, Virgil? Where are they?”

“I don’t know. I just don’t know. We have to hope for the best. They’ll be all right.”

“Will they? Oh, God, will they?”

They sat up most of the night, saying the same things to each other again and again, trying to find a crumb of comfort, trying to believe that the children were being taken care of. Around four in the morning, they went to bed and slept fitfully until the alarm roused them at seven. Rhonda dragged herself into the shower and went downstairs to make breakfast while Virgil showered. Neither of them could eat but they drank some coffee.

Rhonda called Children’s Services and asked for Elsa Mills only to be told Ms. Mills was in a meeting. She tried to explain what she wanted, why she was calling, but the woman wouldn’t tell her anything – just kept saying she would be notified when the hearing would be held.

She and Virge held tightly to their belief in their lawyer. They had both known Herb Thurman for several years and he had done all their legal business for them – wills, trusts for the children, and any legal questions that arose with the business. They looked forward hopefully to seeing him. Herb would know what to do.

Chapter 3

Herb didn't know what to do. He saw them between appointments, since they had none, and was extremely sympathetic but he didn't know what to do. He was a big man, more than six feet tall, with broad shoulders and a prematurely bald head. He was only a few years older than Virgil, who was thirty-six. He sat behind his handsome desk in his high-backed leather swivel chair and shook his head at them.

"I'm sorry," he said, "but I don't handle Children's Services cases. You need a lawyer who specializes in such cases."

"But it's all lies," protested Rhonda. She nodded at the plastic-enclosed note on Herb's desk. "Karen knew Logan had eaten beets the night before. She read that note. Virge found it in her wastebasket, it must have her fingerprints on it. That proves that she knew and that there was no reason to suspect any kind of abuse, much less what she claimed to suspect."

Herb shook his head. "Cases like this don't go

by the same rules of evidence that other criminal cases do. And anyway, the note is not admissible evidence because it was illegally obtained."

"But if I hadn't found it and brought it with me, she would have destroyed it and there wouldn't be any proof."

Herb sighed and leaned forward, speaking earnestly. "It isn't evidence that could ever be used in a courtroom. You had no right to search for it and no right to seize it. You should have gone to the nearest phone and called me."

"And you would have said what? That you don't handle Children's Services cases."

Herb nodded. "But I could have referred you to another counselor who does."

Rhonda's hands were clenched together; she was doing her best not to cry or get emotional. "I don't understand. It's all right for my sister to tell lies and all right for the social worker to take my kids away without notifying us or investigating or anything but it isn't all right for us to get them back?"

"Rhonda, I know how you feel," Herb said, trying to be patient. Trying to be compassionate. "But I can't help you. You need a lawyer who specializes in these cases. I'm not even a criminal lawyer. I only handle business law, tax law, wills, things like that. I have no experience with family law."

"We can't even find out where they are. Whether they're okay. They must be scared and confused. I want my babies back."

Herb twirled his Rolodex and copied a name and phone number on a slip of paper.

"I know you do," he said. "Look, here's the name of a good family lawyer. He does nothing but this kind of legal work. Talk to him and he'll tell you what you need to do."

"Why can't we sue the Children's Services people?" Virgil asked. "They have violated our rights all over the place. Can't we file some kind of suit and force them to give us our kids?"

Herb shook his head. "It doesn't work that way, Virgil. You have to have a lawyer who specializes in family law. You have to go through the process the way it's set up. There aren't any shortcuts. Call this guy and set up an appointment."

He pushed the slip of paper across his desk to Virgil.

Virgil picked it up and stared blankly at it. He looked up and searched Herb's face for some sign of helpful intent. There was none to see. Slowly he got to his feet and held out his hand to Rhonda.

"You, bastard!" she suddenly shrieked. "You don't care. They're not your kids and even if they were you probably still wouldn't care. You don't believe us. You stinking son-of-a-bitch!"

"Rhonda, honey, stop." Virgil tucked the slip of paper into his shirt pocket. "Come on, let's go."

Rhonda burst into tears and let Virgil lead her from the office and out to the car. They were using his car as neither of them could face the Ford with the kids' car seats and toys. Virgil put her inside and went around and got behind the wheel. He made no move to start the engine but let Rhonda cry it out.

"We'll get them back, baby," he said. "Don't worry, we'll get them back."

Gradually, she quieted and finally stopped crying. She mopped up and turned to her husband.

"I'm sorry, Virge. I didn't mean to come unglued like that. I know I'm not making it any easier. Let's find somewhere to call that lawyer. God, I hope he can see us today."

They were unlucky. The lawyer, whose name was Morris Stigleitz, couldn't see them until the following Tuesday. He told Virgil on the phone not to go to Children's Services and not to try to talk to the social worker. Four days to get through. Four days of uncertainty, of dread, of grief, of fear. This, Rhonda thought, is how people feel when their child has been kidnapped.

Rhonda didn't go to the shop the next day. As soon as Virgil left, she started cleaning the house. It was always in pretty good order but she wanted it to be perfect when the children came home.

And, of course, if the social worker wanted to inspect it before releasing the kids, it had to be in absolutely spotless condition. She scrubbed and scoured, polished and burnished. She kept in motion because whenever she stopped the fear took possession of her mind and hammered at her.

That was Friday. Saturday Virgil went to the shop again and Rhonda stayed home. She couldn't stand to be in the house any longer so she went to work on the yard. As it was winter, there wasn't really any gardening to do. She got the ladder and cleaned out the roof gutters. She used the high pressure nozzle on the deck and sidewalks. She backed the Ford out of the garage and went through the boxes stashed on the shelves and under the window. She didn't find much to throw away, they hadn't been there long enough to accumulate much, but she filled a couple of big leaf bags with stuff for the homeless shelter and the Salvation Army. She washed the windows and used the high-pressure nozzle on the cement floor.

She slept a little that night from sheer physical exhaustion. It was the first real sleep she had been able to get since losing her kids. She didn't think Virgil had slept at all. They were both awake before dawn. She went downstairs and made a pot of coffee. Virgil built a fire in the family room and they sat in there to drink it. It should have been a peaceful Sunday morning, getting breakfast that they could eat in a leisurely fashion, playing with the kids, puttering around. Instead, they sat tensely, hunched over their coffee mugs, each feeling alone and scared and cold.

They didn't talk. There was nothing to talk about. They had both said everything it was possible to say, over and over, many times. Now they were emotionally exhausted, operating as automatons.

Virgil took his coffee over to the desk, turned on the computer, and began to get out the income tax records. The sooner they filed, the sooner they'd get back any refund. And they would need cash for the lawyer. It was going to be a long, dreary day. Rhonda decided to go to church. Virgil seldom went and she didn't go every Sunday but she felt it might help. At the very least, it would take up a couple of hours that she didn't know what else to do with.

"I'm going to church, Virge. Want to come with me?"

Virgil looked around blankly. He shook his head, not in a negative way but as if he needed to clear it. "Oh. No, I don't think so. You go ahead."

Rhonda nodded and went upstairs to dress. She showered and made the bed then dressed for church. She wore a royal blue suit with black heels and her silver gray coat with the little mink collar. She almost didn't make it to church; she began to cry when she was halfway there and had to pull over to the curb to get herself under control. It took a few minutes and then a few more to repair her makeup. The congregation was singing when she went in. She slipped into a pew in the very back and took a hymnbook out of the rack. Rather to her surprise, she found she could sing and it felt good to let the words of faith and hope roll out.

Pastor William P. Gillespie preached on the text, "Whosoever shall smite thee on the right cheek, turn to him also thy left." Rhonda had never understood that admonition. If God expected His people to do for themselves and help one another, how did that fit in? She didn't believe He meant for them all to be doormats and allow anyone and everyone to run roughshod over them. So how was she supposed to tell when it was time to turn the other cheek or time to smite back? She quit listening to the Rev. Gillespie and let her thoughts run ahead to the next week.

She knelt, much to the surprise and disapproval of those sitting near enough to see her, and prayed silently and fervently for God to protect her children and return them to her. She explained their needs and her needs and Virge's needs and asked Him rationally and calmly to see justice done and send her children home. She rose and, feeling the Rev. Gillespie and the choir and the congregation irrelevant, left the church. A fresh wave of disapproval followed her but she didn't consciously feel it or see it.

Somehow they made it to Tuesday and their appointment with Morris Stiglitz. It wasn't quite a repeat of their appointment with Herb but it wasn't very helpful or hopeful. Stiglitz explained that there would be a hearing and they would be allowed to present their case.

"What do you mean, our case?" asked Rhonda.

"Your case for getting the children returned to your custody."

"You mean we have to defend ourselves?" she demanded. "We have to give these people reasons why they should give our babies back to us?"

"It isn't right," Virgil put in. "The state has to prove their case against us."

The lawyer was patient. "No, they don't. This isn't a criminal action. At least not yet. This is merely a hearing. Several outcomes are possible, the best scenario would be for the state to return the children to you and monitor you for a few years."

Virgil's jaw was tight as he asked, "And the worst scenario?"

"Would be for the state to turn their evidence over to the District Attorney's office and have you indicted for sexually abusing your daughter. If convicted, you could both go to jail. The children would become permanent wards of the state."

"Oh, God," Rhonda cried. "This can't be happening to us."

"Now, honey," Virgil said, patting her arm. "Easy. We've got to see where we stand. Don't go to pieces on me now."

Rhonda nodded and reached for his hand.

"I understand that a father convicted of such a crime would go to jail and that's where he should be put. But why the mother?"

"Prosecutors don't usually go after the mother in such cases but sometimes they do. If the mother knows about it and doesn't stop it, she's an accomplice and that makes her liable to punishment."

"Please listen," Rhonda asked, fighting for composure. "We are good parents. We love our children. We have never abused them in any way, shape, or form."

"Then that's what the hearing will disclose," Stigleitz stated.

The hearing was scheduled for the next Friday. They could bring in anyone they wanted to speak to their fitness as parents – friends, family, neighbors, teachers. Only there weren't any teachers and they had only lived in their beautiful home for about six months and didn't know any of the neighbors well enough to ask them. Virge's

Mom and Dad would come and tell how great a father their son was. His younger brother Lou would come and bring his wife Lorraine. All the family Rhonda had was Karen. She thought her friend Shirley Warren would stick up for her.

When they got home from Stigleitz' office, Virge sat down in the family room and called his mother.

"Mom, can you and Dad come over here tonight? Or we can come over there, if that would be better."

"What's wrong, Virgil?"

"I'd rather tell you about it face to face."

"Tell me now. So I can think about it before you get here."

"The state has taken the kids away from us."

"The state...what? Who...? Virgil, you aren't making any sense."

"I know. They think we're abusive parents so they went to Karen's and took them away."

"But where did they get that idea in the first place? And where did they take them?"

Virge sighed and passed a hand over his face. He couldn't keep trying to explain to his mother. Hell, he didn't know what it was all about himself.

"Mom, I don't know. I just don't know. We'll come over after dinner, about seven. We'll tell you everything we can then. Okay?"

"Well. Okay. But I don't get it. The whole thing is crazy if you ask me."

"Yes, it is. It's completely insane. Listen, would you call Lou and Lorraine and ask them to come over, too? I can't explain it twice."

"I think it's their bowling night. But I'll call."

"Thanks, Mom."

There was a little more disbelief and a few more questions before he managed to hang up without being rude.

"You shouldn't have told her," Rhonda said. "She'll have it all twisted up by the time she calls Lou and Lorraine."

"I know, but I'm too tired to fight."

"Too tired to fight! We're not talking about the weather here, Virge, we're talking about our kids. If you're already too tired to fight for them, it looks like I'm on my own."

"Rhonda. Calm down. I didn't mean that. You know I didn't mean that."

"Then what did you mean? You said you were too tired to fight and this battle has just started. Don't you want the kids back? Don't you care?"

"For God's sake, Rhonda. Listen to yourself. You're hysterical. Of course I want my kids back. Of course I'll fight for them. But I don't want to fight you and my mother and the whole damn family, too."

"Fine! Now I know where I am. Run from this

if you want to, you always have run from a fight, but I'll fight. I'll fight the whole damn state if I have to. I'll fight for just as long as it takes to get my babies back!"

"You're out of control. Get a grip!"

Rhonda stared at him. She knew she was out of control but she didn't care. She just wanted to scream; to vent her fear and rage.

"You don't care! You didn't even want Griffin. Don't think for a minute that I've forgotten that you wanted me to get an abortion. What kind of father are you? Maybe you did it. Maybe that's how you planned to get rid of them!"

Virge could not bear one more syllable. He put his face very close to hers and said, "Shut up."

The look in his eyes scared her. She got very still and quiet, staring at him.

"Get out," she said, very softly and carefully. "Get out of this house right now."

He took a step toward her. She backed away from him and he took another step toward her. She ran into the kitchen and snatched a knife out of the drawer. She brandished it in front of her. Virgil seized her wrist and squeezed until she let go of the knife.

"No." he said. "This has already gone too far. We're both stressed out of our minds but this is going to stop right here and now."

Rhonda jerked away from him and grabbed her purse from the countertop where she'd plopped it down as she came in the back door. She ran out to her car and locked the doors just as Virge took hold of the handle. He shouted at her to stop and banged the flat of his hand on the window. Her hands shook as she scrabbled in the purse for her keys. She finally found them and managed to get the ignition key in its slot and the car started. He was still yelling as she backed into the street and drove away. Neither saw the tears streaming down the other's face.

Chapter 4

When Virgil got back from his conclave with his family that night, the house was dark. The Ford was in the driveway so he knew Rhonda was home. He didn't know how to face her. The ugly scene between them reverberated in his ears. His family had been less than encouraging.

Lou, his older brother, his only sibling, hadn't said much one way or the other. But his wife Lorraine had said at intervals, "They wouldn't have taken the kids without any reason, Virge."

His parents had been heartsick, as he had expected them to be. As they had been ever since he'd first told them. His dad hadn't said much, just sat in his recliner, hunched forward with his elbows on his knees, looking miserable. His mom had been pretty voluble but there wasn't really very much to say. So she just kept saying the same thing over again, varying the words slightly.

"It will be all right," she'd said. "God won't let anything bad happen to the children."

He had pointed out that God had already let

something bad happen to the children but it had no effect on her faith that God would not let harm come to children. He knew it would be useless to show her news articles about raped, murdered, and abused children. She lived in her own reality and the facts be damned.

He had understood when he left his parents' modest little home, the home he had grown up in, that there would be no help from his family. None of them had any resources to draw on as far as hiring a lawyer went and it was evident that there wouldn't be much in the way of emotional support, either.

Virge went through the darkened kitchen and up the stairs without turning on any lights. Rhonda was not in their bedroom, nor the bathroom. Then where was she? Sleeping on the sofa in the family room? In one of the kids' rooms? He flicked the switch to turn on the lights in the upper hall. There was no bed in Logan's room, only a crib. She must be in Griffin's room. He opened the door quietly, so as not to startle her, but she wasn't there. He opened the door to Logan's room.

Rhonda was sitting in the rocking chair, cradling Logan's big cloth dolly, slowly rocking back and forth. She looked up at him but didn't speak.

Virge stood with his hand on the doorknob.

"Rhonda?" he ventured. "Rhonda, I'm sorry. You don't know how sorry I am."

Rhonda looked away.

"Don't do this, Rhonda. We have to work together to get our kids back. We can't let the stress tear us apart from each other."

"There doesn't seem to be much to say," she said.

"Come on downstairs and I'll make some coffee or pour some wine or something. We need to talk."

Rhonda put the dolly in Logan's crib and went down the stairs. Virge followed her to the family room. She sat in her favorite chair, legs curled so her feet were on the seat, and waited.

"Would you rather have coffee or wine?" Virgil asked.

"I don't want anything. Just tell me what there is to talk about."

Virge sat down in his favorite chair, hunched forward, elbows on his knees, gazing at his wife as if he was trying to classify her.

"Well," he said at last, "Mom thinks everything will be all right. Lorraine thinks I'm guilty and Lou just shakes his head."

"I'm not surprised. Lorraine has always been incredibly stupid. What on earth your brother ever saw in her is more than I can imagine. What about your dad? What does he think?"

"I don't know. He hardly opened his mouth all evening."

"This discussion didn't take long. I'm going back upstairs."

"Wait, Rhonda. We need to make plans."

"Plans?" Rhonda laughed. "Plans, Virge? How can we possibly make any plans? Our kids are gone. We don't know when or even if we'll get them back. What kind of plans can we make?"

"We can plan how we're going to attack the problem."

"The problem." Rhonda laughed again. Abruptly, she stood up. Her jaw was set and her rage vibrated in her voice. "Okay, call it a problem. Just like school – a train was traveling east at a hundred and eighty miles an hour and a car was traveling west at sixty-eight miles an hour. How long before they have a head-on collision with no survivors? How about that for a problem?"

She whirled around and ran up the stairs. Virgil heard a door slam shut. He went over to the computer and turned it on. While it was warming up, he went to the kitchen for a glass of merlot. He sat down and punched up the Internet and began to search for sites that dealt with situations like his.

He typed "child abuse" in the search box. Three million, five hundred eighty-nine thousand, four hundred seventy sites. 3,589,470. In the next four hours Virge learned dozens of ways to abuse a child that he had never heard of before. That he wished he had not heard of now. Where were his children? His darling baby girl and his wondrous little boy. They had known only love and gentleness in a clean, nurturing home. He had almost said safe home. He and Rhonda had thought it was safe. They had taken good care of their babies. Fed them right, guarded them, read them stories, played with them. Had eschewed day care centers where strangers would teach and care for their precious little ones. Rhonda had stayed home with them until Logan was a year old and when she went to work at the pharmacy, she had gotten her sister to babysit.

You could count on family. Only now they had found that they couldn't. He and Karen had never liked one another but that hadn't seemed to matter when they needed a babysitter. Karen loved Logan and Griffin. She could be depended on to take good care of them. She had, too. Until the day she turned them over to the state. As it had innumerable times since that day, Virgil's mind began to run the circuit of what happened, through anguished cries of "why?", and then to fury and terror at where the children were and what was happening to them. His research gave him new possibilities to worry about, new pictures to torture himself with. He went out to the kitchen.

He had finished the wine but he thought there was a bottle of bourbon in the cupboard over the refrigerator. There was. He took it down and poured a couple of ounces in a glass and filled the glass with crushed ice and water from the dispenser in the refrigerator door. He went back to the family room and sat back down at the computer.

When Rhonda came downstairs at seven the next morning, Virgil was asleep on the couch. She said his name a couple of times and when he didn't respond, she went over and shook him by the shoulder.

"Virgil. Time to get up. Come on, get up."

He shook her hand off and muttered something she didn't understand.

"Virgil! Get up!"

His eyes opened blearily. "What? What's the matter?"

Rhonda stepped back from his breath. Then she saw the empty glass on the coffee table and the bourbon bottle on the floor. She picked it up and held it to the light. It was less than half full.

"How much of this did you drink last night?" she asked.

Virge sat up and swung his feet to the floor. He sat hunched up, his elbows on his knees, his face in his hands.

"How much, Virgil? How much did you drink last night?"

He look up at her, suddenly angry. "Just as much as it took to let me sleep!"

"You got drunk and now you're hung over," she said nastily. "Too bad. It's time to get dressed and go to work."

"Don't tell me what to do."

"It looks like someone's got to."

"Listen, this whole thing is your fault so you can just quit nagging me."

"My fault?"

Rhonda was astounded. It was a horrible situation but she didn't see how it could be blamed on her. For that matter, she didn't see how it could be blamed on anyone except Karen and the so-called social worker who had kidnapped her kids. She was about to say so when Virge spoke again.

"Yes, your fault. You insisted you had to come back to work. You couldn't stay home and take care of the kids, you needed something more stimulating to do. Then nothing would do but you had to get your sister to babysit." His voice went falsetto, in a sort of sing-song whine, "Karen loves Logan and Griffie, she'll take better care of them than strangers at a daycare center." He went back to his own voice. "I hope you're satisfied with the way Karen took care of them. Are you, Rhonda?"

Virgil stood up and she stepped back several steps at the violence she saw in his face, suddenly afraid of her husband. He laughed meanly.

"Are you? How do you like how your sister took care of the kids?"

Her silence enraged him.

"Are you happy now?"

"Virgil, stop it!" she cried. "Stop!"

He turned and went up the stairs. She heard the door of the master bedroom close. She went into the kitchen and opened the door of the refrigerator. There wasn't much there. She got out a jar of peach jam and made herself a couple of peanut butter and jam sandwiches. She wished she had some potato chips. She opened a can of pineapple juice and poured a glass, then took it into the family room and sat staring out the window while she ate.

She was still there when Virgil came downstairs dressed for the shop.

"Well," he said, "I thought you said it was time to go to work."

"It is," she answered, without looking at him.

"Then why aren't you ready?"

"I'll be there in a little bit."

"You'd better not be late. And after this you ride with me. There's no sense in running both cars every day when you don't have to drop off the kids or pick them up."

When the door had closed behind him, Rhonda began to cry. Everything was ruined. Her life was in tatters. Her family was destroyed and her husband acted like he hated her. She cried for a long time. When her tears were exhausted, she mopped up and glanced at the clock over the fireplace. Nine-thirty. Mr. Stigleitz ought to be in his office. She rummaged around in the desk until she found his card. She sat down and took a deep breath then pressed his number on the telephone keypad. To her intense disappointment, although not to her surprise, the secretary wouldn't put her through to the lawyer. There was a lot of doubletalk about how he was in a meeting and due in court and would call her as soon as he had anything fresh to tell her. Rhonda put the phone down. He wasn't going to call. Her babies were gone forever.

She thought about Children's Services and how she could approach them to find out where the children were. She turned the computer on and pulled up the state website. It took her quite a long time to find Children's Services but once on the right page, she found an incredible amount of information. Elsa Mills was listed in the employee directory and there was even a brief bio of her with a picture. It gave her husband's name, Paul, and even gave her children's names and ages: Zuzie, 14; Fern, 13; and Paul, Jr. 10. She bookmarked the site and pulled up the white pages to find the family's address. 21579 Peach Orchard Court. She made a note of the address and phone number.

Rhonda had never before used the computer to locate a person and was astounded at how easy it was. All that information just sitting there for the taking. What else could she find out? She looked for a site that would list school districts and the schools in each one. It took a little while but she finally figured out which schools served Peach Orchard Court and printed the pages with their names and addresses and phone numbers. What else? Blogs. She had barely heard of blogs but she did know that kids often posted their thoughts and activities on their blogs. Maybe Zuzie Mills did. Rhonda typed the name in the search box. She tried for quite a long time but finally had to give up for the day. She would try again another time.

It was nearly noon when Rhonda finally got to the shop. She went behind the counter and when Virge finished with his customer he went back to work dispensing medications. Customers kept her busy through the lunch hour so she opened a bag of bite-size candy and popped one in her mouth whenever the opportunity arose.

At the end of the day, Rhonda stopped and

picked up pizza for dinner. But Virgil's Plymouth wasn't there when she pulled into the driveway. He still hadn't come home by the time she decided to go to bed, back in the master bedroom. She finished the pizza and took the box out to the trash can. Virge made a little racket when he finally did come home. Rhonda looked at the bedside clock. Two-forty-seven A.M.

Virge turned on the bathroom light and undressed. He didn't turn it off before he got into bed so Rhonda got up and flicked the switch. She was wide awake by that time so she went downstairs. She sat in the dark in the family room, her mind replaying the loss of her kids, the useless visits to the attorneys' offices, the rage she felt toward Karen and the whole rotten system that could destroy people so easily, so relentlessly, so callously. Where were they? Where was little Griffin? Four years old, shocked and bewildered to be torn from his family. And Logan. Just a baby. Just beginning to walk, just beginning to say a few little words. Rhonda hoped they had at least let her keep her stuffed rabbit.

She cried for a long time. The pain was overwhelming. Besides the children, something was happening to her and Virge. She wanted to remain close to him to comfort him and be comforted by him but it wasn't working that way. She was angry with him. It was irrational and she knew it but there it was – a cold knot of anger at her husband. The whole thing was his fault somehow. She knew he had done nothing wrong. He was a good father and he loved his children. But he was the one they accused. If it weren't for him, she would still have her babies.

Her tears ceased at last and she became aware that she was thirsty. She went into the kitchen and poured herself a glass of Squirt over ice. Putting the soda bottle back in the refrigerator, she saw some left over potato salad. She got a fork and took it and the salad and soda back into the family room with her. She turned on a lamp and curled up on the couch with a Bernie Rhodenbarr murder mystery that she had read before.

She wasn't really reading, though. Once the potato salad was gone, she drifted into thinking about Elsa Mills. God damn the woman to hell. She had her three kids, safe and secure. No one was going to come and yank them away from her. She was even going to have another baby. It wasn't fair. It was not fair. The woman could come into your home and take your children with one lying statement from a total stranger to her, with no evidence whatsoever, with no investigation into the circumstances. She could just come in and take your children. And you couldn't do a thing to get them back. You couldn't even find out where they were, if they were all right. How many families had she wrecked? How many children had she kidnapped? How many parents had she destroyed? What if someone did that to her? But no one would. Elsa Mills was a perpetrator, not a victim. None of her co-workers would dare to intervene even if they knew she or her husband abused their children. Elsa would know too much about how the system works to be caught in it. God damn her soul.

Chapter 5

Morris Stigleitz, the family law specialist, had impressed on both Virgil and Rhonda that they must remain calm and reasonable at all costs. Any show of nervousness or emotion would work against them. The social workers would consider it a sign of instability. He especially cautioned them against any manifestation of anger. Anger is anathema to social workers who are protecting children from their parents. Consequently, Rhonda was so nervous about appearing nervous that she couldn't keep her hands or her voice from shaking. Afterwards she remembered very little of the hearing, mostly that the woman who appeared to be the boss was in an advanced stage of pregnancy and seemed to have already made up her mind about the outcome.

Virgil was in a sullen rage and could hardly be prevailed upon to answer questions at all, much less project a calm and reasonable demeanor. His parents were there, his mother twittering with anxiety, his father stolidly silent. Rhonda had succeeded in getting Lou and Lorraine to stay away but the state had brought Karen in. Rhonda's best friend, Shirley Warren, had sent a letter but couldn't attend, being out of town at a cosmetic sales convention. Pastor Gillespie had also sent a letter, which was all Rhonda had asked him for. She wasn't sure he knew them well enough to speak on their behalf.

At the appointed time, Rhonda and Virge and the others were shown into a room and seated around a conference table. A few minutes later three women came in and sat together at one end. The pregnant one, Elsa Mills, introduced herself and the other two but Rhonda was never able to recall their names or anything about them. They said little, merely making occasional notes. Elsa had a clipboard and a pen, which she placed on the table in front of herself.

"Mr. Stigleitz, perhaps you will introduce your clients and these other folks," Elsa suggested.

He did so and Elsa explained that this was an informal hearing for the purpose of determining what was best for the two children, Griffin and Logan Thwait.

"Children's Services received a report that Logan Thwait, then seventeen months old, had been sexually abused by her father, Virgil Thwait. The children were in the custody of their maternal aunt, Karen Mulligan. Mrs. Mulligan reported that she had been suspicious for some time and when she found blood in the baby's diaper, she knew the children needed protection and called this office. Mrs. Mulligan, is that substantially what happened?"

Karen started to speak and caught Virgil's eye. She quailed before the look of contempt and loathing he focused on her. Elsa looked at him and made a check mark and short note on her clipboard.

"Mrs. Mulligan?" she prompted.

"No, I…it was a mistake. I was wrong."

"Mrs. Mulligan, we are not here to try Mr. Thwait or to prove his innocence or guilt. Please answer my question. As I stated it a moment ago, were those the actions you took in regard to Logan Thwait?"

Karen looked at her sister, pleading with her, but met only frozen blankness. She looked down at her hands on the table. "Yes."

"Thank you, Mrs. Mulligan." Elsa made a couple more check marks on her clipboard. "Mr. Thwait, you've been accused of a heinous act, do you want to make a statement?"

Virgil braced himself, gripping his hands together and clamping his jaw hard. When he had himself under control, he spoke. "My daughter and son are more precious to me than life itself. I would never do anything to harm either one of them. My wife had given the baby beets for supper the night before this happened. The red in her diaper was beets, not blood." He took the plastic encased note out of his jacket pocket and handed it to Elsa. "That is a note that I wrote to Karen and left in the diaper bag."

Elsa frowned at it. "There is no indication that Mrs. Mulligan saw the note or that it was ever in the diaper bag."

"I found it in her wastepaper basket that night, when my wife and I went to talk to her. She as good as admitted that she had read it."

"Mrs. Mulligan, did you read this note? Did you know that Mr. Thwait claimed the red was beets, not blood?"

"No, I never saw the note. I didn't know anything about his claim it was beets until he and Rhonda came to my house that night. They were both mad and Rhonda threatened to kill me."

"Indeed." Elsa made another check mark and an explanatory paragraph in the margin. "Mrs. Thwait, do you wish to add anything?"

"Virgil is telling the truth. He's a good father. He would never hurt either of the children. He is not the kind of man to sexually abuse anyone, especially not his own baby girl. Please, give our children back to us."

Rhonda had to stop speaking, she was nearly overwhelmed with emotion and struggling to conceal it. Elsa nodded and made another check mark.

"I have here a couple of letters, one from a friend and one from the Thwaits' pastor. It's unfortunate that they couldn't come to this hearing. However, their letters in support of the Thwaits will be taken into consideration. Does anyone else want to make a statement?"

Virgil's mother raised her hand. Elsa nodded at her.

"Go ahead, Mrs…"

"Thwait. I'm Virgil's mother so my name is Thwait. Tricia Thwait. This is his father, Leroy Thwait."

"You want to say something, Mrs. Thwait?"

"Yes, I do. I want to say that my son, Virgil there, is a good man. He was a good boy and now he's a good man. I don't care what that fat slob of a sister-in-law says, Virgil would never do such a thing. Never."

"Shut up!" Karen stood up and literally quivered with rage.

Rhonda thought how ridiculous she looked, like Santa, a right jolly old elf, who shook when he laughed, in spite of himself. She could feel herself getting hysterical and tried hard to keep a grip on herself.

"Don't you tell me to shut up," Tricia shot back, getting to her feet. "You started this mess.

You're a liar and God will strike you dead where you stand."

Leroy put his hand on Tricia's arm and gently tugged. She looked down at him and he shook his head at her. She shot a look of vicious hatred at Karen but sat down without saying anything more.

Elsa stood, leaning backward to compensate for the extra weight of the baby in front. "I think we've heard enough. Thank you all for coming. Mr. & Mrs. Thwait, we'll be in touch."

"But, what about my babies?" Rhonda cried. "When are my babies coming home?"

Elsa gave Stigleitz a look that he had no trouble interpreting as meaning it was up to him to explain to his clients how the system worked.

Rhonda was rushing to catch up with Elsa; the lawyer hurried around the table to intercept her.

"Wait," Rhonda begged. "Please, tell me where they are. Are they all right? Who is taking care of them? They must be upset. Please, where are they?"

Elsa didn't even look around at her.

Stigleitz grasped her right arm and a moment later Virge took her left one. They held her as she struggled to break free, crying now.

"Rhonda," Virge said. "Get a grip. This won't help."

"Virgil is right," Stigleitz said. "Calm down,

Rhonda. Take it easy."

Karen put on her coat and gathered up her purse and gloves and went out without looking at her sister.

Leroy and Tricia got ready to go and paused to say a few words to Virgil as they left.

Virgil got Rhonda quieted enough to put her coat on and Stigleitz walked them to their car. Rhonda never knew what he said to Virge, she was too upset to hear.

Chapter 6

Virgil fumbled for the snooze button when the alarm went off and finally succeeded in pressing it in just the right spot to make the alarm quit buzzing. The third time the buzzing started he turned the alarm off and lay looking up at the ceiling. He felt terrible. His head ached and his mouth was sticky and thick. He looked over at Rhonda. Tenderness welled up toward her. She looked so sweet, sleeping on her side. He turned on his side to face her and took her hand in his. She opened her eyes and smiled at him. His heart fluttered and he smiled back. This is how it used to be, how it should be. He would move heaven and earth to get them back to this loving feeling permanently. If they worked together, they would get their kids back and everything would be good again.

"Rhonda," he said. "Oh, Rhonda."

He started to pull her to him, to enfold her in his love. There was so much he wanted to tell her. So much he wanted her to tell him. She jerked away from him violently as last night's whiskey blasted into her face. The revulsion of her expression startled, then enraged him.

Rhonda flung herself out of bed and reached for her muumuu. It was deep blue with pink and yellow hibiscus blossoms scattered over it in a pattern so cheerful that it seemed a deliberate affront to her mood and Virgil's. As she slipped it over her nightgown, he saw that her figure had thickened. She had always had to watch her weight and was touchy about his occasional teasing.

"You're getting fat," he said.

"At least I'm not a drunk," she countered.

"Neither am I," he said. "A few drinks now and then doesn't make me a drunk."

"No, of course not. You're so hungover right this minute that you can hardly see straight. If you can see straight."

She went into the bathroom and slammed the door. Virgil sat on the side of the bed and fumed. When Rhonda came out, she was already regretting her words. But she wasn't yet ready to apologize.

"You'd better lay off the candy," he said. "Or you'll look just like Karen."

That was one of her hot buttons and well he knew it.

"Well, you'd better lay off the booze or you'll

end up with your head in the gutter."

She was out the door and halfway down the stairs before he found words again. He dragged himself into the shower and when he was dressed and got himself downstairs, he found that his wife had cooked him breakfast. He looked distastefully at the plate she thrust at him. Bacon in a puddle of grease, underdone fried eggs when she knew he could only eat them hard boiled. Just looking at that plate of food made him queasy.

"Here," she said. "Sit down and eat."

"No, thanks," he said. "Is there any coffee?"

"No, I haven't had time to make any. I've been too busy getting your breakfast. You'd better get something on your stomach. You'll feel better when you've eaten."

Virge pushed the plate away. "Rhonda, I don't want this crap. You know I can't eat raw eggs. Get it out of my face."

"Fine. I'll get it out of your face."

She slammed the plate on the floor. It shattered and grease and egg yolk splattered all over the kitchen. All over Virge's slacks and Rhonda's muumuu, too.

"You stupid bitch. What's wrong with you?"

"Me? What's wrong with me? What's wrong with you?"

Virgil whirled and went back upstairs. He took a couple more headache tablets and changed his slacks. When he got back to the kitchen, Rhonda was sitting at the table, her head on her out flung arms sobbing, the mess still on the floor.

"Are you coming to the store today?" Virge demanded.

She didn't look up. "I don't know. Maybe."

"It would be better if you'd stay home and clean the place up. You haven't even put dishes in the dishwasher for a week or more. It's a pigpen."

Rhonda lifted her head and groped in her pocket for a tissue. "Get out of here! If you'd do your part, maybe I would feel like doing mine. Just get out now."

"Gladly."

Virgil slammed out the back door and Rhonda put her head down and cried. Cried for herself, for her kids, for her marriage. Everything had turned bad. Without her kids life wasn't worth living. She thought about suicide. It would be easy enough to take some pills from the pharmacy. It would be done before Virge noticed they were gone. But that would mean that when the kids came home, they would be motherless. They were already motherless, she couldn't make it final. Besides her religious beliefs precluded suicide. She would have to stick it out. The years of life seemed to stretch in front of her endlessly. Dreary, hopeless, joyless years. Finally, her tears dried up and she wearily dragged herself up and set about cleaning the house. It was nearly noon and she was just putting the vacuum cleaner away when Karen came in the back door.

Rhonda was outraged. "What the hell do you mean, barging in here like you owned the place? Get out."

"You're still in your muumuu? It's almost noon. Rhonda, you're a mess."

"Go away."

"If you don't take better care of yourself, Virge is going to start looking around at other women. You have to keep yourself up for a man."

"Karen, just go away. You've caused enough trouble." Rhonda was keeping herself in check with an effort.

"I know you're mad at me, Rhonda, and I don't really blame you. But I want to see the kids."

"*You* want to see the kids? So do I. So does Virgil. We don't even know where Griffin and Logan are!"

"You mean they're not here? You mean...What do you mean?"

"I mean the state still has them. I mean because of your lies the state has taken my babies and I don't know where they are."

Karen collapsed into a chair at the kitchen table. "But that's not what was supposed to happen."

Rhonda sat down opposite her sister. “Oh. It isn’t. Okay, Karen, you tell me what was supposed to happen.”

“I had no idea they would keep the kids. I thought they would investigate for a couple of days and you’d get them back.”

“And why did you think that was a good idea?”

“I didn’t. I mean I didn’t think it was exactly a good idea, I just thought...”

Karen flinched from the fury in Rhonda’s eyes.

“You just thought. Karen, you are a piece of shit. I’ve always known that but I thought after we both grew up and were adults that we could get along and maybe learn to be sisters. Virge didn’t want me to get you to babysit but you seemed to love them and I thought you would take good care of them. Oh, God!”

“I did take good care of them, Rhonda. I did.”

“Oh, yes, you took such good care of them that they’re gone now. Do you know where they are? Do you have any idea? Because the Children’s Services people won’t tell me anything. They won’t even let me send their favorite toys to them. So do you know where Griffie and Logan are?”

“No, of course not.”

“Then I guess you didn’t take such good care of them, did you?”

"I did. I love your kids. I would never do anything to hurt them."

"What's wrong with you?" Rhonda screamed. She stumbled to the door and yanked it open. "You are completely crazy. You are nuts!"

"I came to apologize," Karen said.

"Apologize! Apologize? My God. You've destroyed my family."

"I'm sorry, Rhonda. Can't you see how sorry I am? Can't you have some compassion for me?"

"You want me to feel sorry for you? You are incredibly stupid. Get out of here before I murder you."

"Rhonda, let me help you..."

Rhonda's voice was soft as she said, "I will kill you if you aren't out of here in ten seconds."

Karen was frightened then. She almost believed that her sister meant what she said. She scuttled out the door and into her car, locking the door before she started the engine.

Adrenaline kept Rhonda going while she locked the back door and went upstairs to shower and get dressed for the store. She decided to skip lunch. Virge was right, she was putting on weight and seeing Karen had reminded her how much she didn't want to look like her sister.

At the store, she put her coat and purse in the office back of the drug counter and went up to the front. Virge was busy at the cash register with three people waiting to pay for their purchases. Another customer was standing at the drug counter, waiting to be helped. Virge handed a woman her change and her little bag of purchases, smiled at her as he thanked her, then turned to Rhonda and glared at her.

As Virge went back to the drug counter, Rhonda smiled at the next customer in line and began to ring up his items. They stayed busy through the lunch hour then things slacked off a little.

"I'm going out for lunch," Virge said. "I'll be back in twenty minutes, half-an-hour."

He headed for the front door.

"You should wear your coat," Rhonda said. "It's cold out."

"I'm just going to the cafe down the block," he said impatiently.

Virge's mention of lunch reminded Rhonda that she was hungry. She opened a bag of potato chips and ate them quickly, then stuffed the empty bag under some other papers in the trash basket. The nutritive value of potato chips being pretty much nil, except for the fat, she was still hungry. She glanced guiltily at the door then opened a bag of miniature candy bars. She ate three before a customer came in but munched on them all afternoon, desperately trying to fill the emptiness, trying to feel something besides pain.

At the end of the day, she and Virge locked up and balanced the cash drawer. Virge was making up the bank deposit while Rhonda put her coat on.

"I'll go ahead and get dinner started," she said.

"Don't wait for me. I'll probably be late," he said, trying to sound matter-of-fact.

"Why? Where are you going?"

"Just don't wait dinner for me." He clenched his jaw, knowing that she wouldn't let his statement alone.

"You're not going out drinking, are you?" she asked hesitantly.

"Look, you're not my mother, you don't have to know where I am every minute, twenty-four-seven."

"Virge, I know I haven't been doing everything I should, but we need to work through this together. Don't get to drinking. Please."

"There isn't anything to work through, Rhonda. You need to get real and face the fact that we're not going to get the kids back."

Rhonda burst into tears. "Don't say that. Don't say that, Virge. The state can't keep them. We haven't done anything wrong. The law's on our side."

"For God's sake!" Virgil shook his head disgustedly. "The law is not on our side! The law doesn't even matter. The state took the kids and the state's going to keep them. Right and wrong have nothing to do with it. The law has nothing to do with it."

"But, that can't be right. If we haven't done anything wrong, the law is supposed to protect us. To protect our children. Virge, we just have to give the lawyer a little time to work his way through the system."

"Stop sniveling, Rhonda. It's not going to happen. The kids are not going to come home."

Suddenly Rhonda lost her temper. "You son of a bitch. You don't care. You're exactly like those people from Children's Services. You're like the lawyers. You don't care if you never see Logan and Griffin again. Go on, then. Go on and get drunk. Stay drunk for the rest of your life."

Virgil gave her a look of loathing and slammed out the back door. Rhonda ran out but was only in time to see him screech the tires in his rush to get away from her.

When she got home, there were no lights on in the house. She went upstairs, ran a tubful of hot water, and soaked for a long time. She was reading in bed, munching on a bag of chocolate chips when she heard the back door close noisily. She grabbed her robe and went to the head of the stairs.

"Virge?" she called. "Is that you?"

Virgil was standing at the foot of the stairs, looking blankly up at her. He started up the stairs, missed the bottom step a couple of times and abruptly sat down on it.

Drunk as a skunk, she diagnosed disgustedly. She turned and went into Griffin's room, hoping that Virge wouldn't throw up on the stairs. Or in the bed, supposing he ever managed to get that far.

The next morning she awoke feeling as if a heavy pall were pressing down on her. Sunshine streamed in the window, it was a beautiful day. She wished it were raining. She picked her watch up from the floor where she'd placed it beside the bed. Almost seven o'clock. Might as well get up and face the day.

She got up very quietly, not yet ready to deal with Virgil. She had a bad headache. Opening her purse to get some aspirin, she saw the candy she had put there the day before. Two big bags of miniature bars. She opened one bag and ate a couple of the little bars then hid one bag in a dresser drawer under Griffin's t-shirts. She hid the other bag in his closet, on the shelf, behind a stack of Little Golden Books. She took four aspirin into the hall bathroom for water with which to swallow them. She hoped Virgil wouldn't wake until she was dressed and had her shoes on. She always felt unprotected without her shoes. She moved silently into the master bedroom and was astonished not to find Virgil in bed. It was just as she'd left it the night before. Her book was even still face down by her pillow. Well, maybe her husband was ashamed to face her. Or maybe he was downstairs, in the throes of a killer hangover.

She pulled a black pantsuit out of the closet and fresh underwear out of her dresser and went into the bathroom. She locked the door and stripped. There was a full-length mirror on the back of the door; against her will she saw the little roll of fat on her midriff. It intensified her feeling of hollow anxiety.

Showered, dressed, and shod, she went back to Griffin's room for her purse. She took a couple more candies out of her stash and ate them on her way down the stairs. She was nearly at the bottom when she glanced into the family room and saw Virgil on the couch. Abandoning her intention to have a wholesome breakfast before leaving for the store, she scurried out the back door and into her car.

There was an old-fashioned coffee shop near the store and she stopped there for breakfast. Bacon and scrambled eggs with hash browns and an English muffin. Orange juice and coffee. Her stomach was full but she hadn't made a dent in the hollow feeling.

Chapter 7

At the Children's Services office, Elsa Mills was sitting at her desk reading a report. She'd had to stop and think a minute before she remembered the circumstances of the case. The little boy and girl at a relative's house and a bloody diaper from the father molesting the girl. She shook her head. As always, she was incredulous at the terrible things people inflicted on their innocent babies. As she read, she slowly rubbed her palm over her own baby. Just two weeks from term, he was a kicker. Even without the sonogram, she would have known it was a boy by the vigorous way he kicked. Neither of her girls had kicked like that but her other boy had.

Elsa glanced at her watch. It was almost five and she was tired and her back ached. She would leave a few minutes early, maybe miss the worst of the rush hour traffic. She took her purse out of her bottom desk drawer and folded the report and stuck it in the purse. She would finish reading it at home, where she could put her feet up and relax.

She was halfway to the door when she went back to her cubicle and gathered up an armload of folders to take home. On the way out she told the receptionist that she would be working at home the next day.

She hadn't left work early enough to miss any of the rush hour traffic and by the time she got home, she was completely frazzled. She dropped her folders and her purse on the credenza in the foyer and kicked off her shoes. She hung her coat in the hall closet and went to the kitchen. Her thirteen-year-old daughter was sitting at the kitchen table working on some kind of art project. Some very messy project involving papier-mâché, paste, and lots of strips of crepe paper.

"Hi, Mom."

"Hi, Fern. What are you making?"

Elsa filled the tea kettle and set it on the burner to heat.

"It's a piñata. A giraffe."

"I see. Well, no sense making it too easy on yourself. Where's your sister?"

"Zuzie? Zuzie's over at Carolyn's house. She's having a slumber party."

"And Paulie?"

"I think he's upstairs but he might be playing video games in the family room."

"Go get him, will you?"

"Mom, I'm a little busy here. Can't you just

yell for him?"

"Fern, go get your brother. I'm tired and I'm in no mood for any back talk."

Fern threw her mother an annoyed glance but went to do as she was bid. The teakettle whistled and Elsa made herself a mug of tea and took it into the family room. She settled herself on the couch with her feet up and sipped her tea. Sounds of altercation filtered down the stairs and she sighed. A couple of minutes later Fern and ten-year-old Paulie came clattering down the stairs and into the room.

"Whatcha want, Mom?" Paulie asked.

"Your dad is going to be late tonight; he's got a basketball game across town, so we're all going to make our own dinner."

"Aw, Mom, c'mon. I can't cook," Paulie protested.

"You don't have to cook, there's plenty of stuff for sandwiches and there's cole slaw. I think there's some macaroni salad, too. Or you can heat up some soup or chili. I'm tired and I don't feel like cooking anything."

"Why can't Zuzie make dinner?"

"She's not here. She's spending the night at Carolyn's."

"Well, why can't Fern do it?"

"Oh, no, you don't!" Fern quickly countered. "I can't cook, either."

"Listen," Elsa said, "you can just quit moaning and groaning about it. If you're going to get anything to eat tonight, you're going to fix it yourselves."

She picked up the remote control and flicked the TV on, flipping through the channels to find something watchable. Paulie sulked for a few minutes then went out to the kitchen where Fern was back at work on her piñata. Elsa could hear them fussing at each other but it wasn't long before Paulie went upstairs carrying a well-laden plate, a bag of corn chips, and a glass of milk.

Elsa watched the tail end of a rather grim movie in which all the actors looked grungy, sweaty and badly clothed. The plot was rather vague but everyone got beaten up and quite a few got shot. She hoped the good guys won but wasn't sure which ones they were. She turned the TV off when she heard her husband come in the front door and go into the kitchen where he exchanged greetings with Fern. She made room for him beside her and he wandered in and sat down, giving her a quick kiss and putting his hand on the baby.

"I saw the pile of folders on the credenza," he said. "I hope it means you're going to work here tomorrow and not that you're going to be most of the night working."

"No, I decided to work at home tomorrow."

"Good." He settled back and rubbed his forehead.

"Tough day?"

"Huh? Oh. No, it was okay."

"I thought maybe you had a headache."

Paul smiled at her. "No, I'm fine. As a matter of fact, I'm great. We won the game, forty-seven to thirty-four."

Elsa smiled at him. "Good for you. Who did you play? Not your arch rivals, the Trojans?"

"Well, no. But it was almost as good. We beat the pants off the Scorpions."

"That must feel good, considering that they've beaten your pants off the last four or five times you've played them."

Paul shot her a look. "Yeah, well, it did feel good. So good I took the kids out for pizza after the game."

"Good. There's nothing to eat here."

"Where is everybody?"

"Well, you saw Fern in the kitchen. Paulie's upstairs in his room. Zuzie's at a sleepover at Carolyn's."

"No, she's not. Carolyn and her whole family were at the game and Zuzie wasn't with them."

"Maybe she..."

Paul went to the desk and grabbed the phone. He plopped down in an easy chair to dial. "Wayne? This is Paul Mills. Is Zuzie there?" He listened a moment. “Could I speak to Carolyn? Thanks.” He shook his head at Elsa and waited for Carolyn to come on the line. “Carolyn? This is Zuzie’s dad. Do you know where she is?” He paused to listen. “No, we thought she was with you. You’re not having a sleepover tonight?” He asked a couple more futile questions and pushed the disconnect button. He put the phone back on the desk and sat back down.

“They don’t know where she is?” Elsa asked.

“No idea. No sleepover there or anywhere else that Carolyn knows of. Who told you she was with Carolyn?”

“Fern. Get her in here, will you? Let’s get to the bottom of this.”

Fern came in, looking a little scared and a little defiant. “All right, I heard you. Zuzie asked me to tell you she was staying at Carolyn’s tonight. That’s all I know.”

“You lied for her?” Elsa was outraged. “Just like that? Zuzie asked you to lie to your parents and you did it. No problem, it’s just your parents. Do you know where she is? Or who she’s with? Or when she’ll be home? Did it ever occur to you that it’s dangerous for a young girl to be wandering around town on her own?”

Fern was trying to speak and when Elsa finally had to stop for breath, she said, “Mom. She’s not just wandering around town...”

Elsa interrupted. "No? Then where is she? You'd better speak up and you'd better tell the truth."

"Mom, I am telling the truth. I haven't lied to you."

"Oh, really? Your dad called Carolyn's house. There is no sleepover. Zuzie is not there."

"Well, I didn't know that."

"Fern, I swear to God, if you don't start telling me the truth, I'm going to lose my temper with you."

"Wait a minute," Paul interjected. "Just calm down. This doesn't have to be a four-act play."

"Calm down!" Elsa's rage was growing. "Your daughter is out God knows where, with God knows who and you're not concerned? All you can say is calm down? Fern, I want to know where Zuzie is and I want to know now."

"I don't know, Mom. I thought she was at Carolyn's."

"No, you didn't. You knew she was sneaking off somewhere else. Is she with that Conroy kid? Because if she is, she's going to regret it."

Paul tried again. "Elsa, stop it. Just stop it. Fern hasn't done anything wrong and you don't know what Zuzie's doing. Come on, honey, why don't you go upstairs and have a nice, long, relaxing bath and I'll go find Zuzie?"

He jerked his head at Fern as he spoke and she

took the hint and went back to the kitchen.

Elsa took a long breath. “I’m sorry. It’s just...I see so many horrors with kids that it spooks me when don’t know where mine are. You’re right, I’m overreacting.”

Paul smiled at her. “That’s better. I’ll start with the phone and let my fingers do the walking. She’ll be at one of her girlfriend’s, doing homework or playing video games or something equally innocuous.”

Elsa smiled back at him and started up the stairs. A few steps up she leaned over the baluster and called, “Just the same, when she gets home, I’m going to ground her!”

Paul found her after an hour or so. She was with a bunch of kids at a friend’s house all right but the friend was a boy and his parents weren’t home. There was beer but Paul believed his daughter when she said she hadn’t had any. He brought her home, giving her a good talking to in the car on the way and sending her to her room as soon as they entered the house. He kept Elsa distracted enough that she didn’t get to talk to Zuzie, thus averting a major mother-daughter blowup. Things settled back to normal. But Elsa went into labor in the middle of the night and the baby was born at 3:49 A.M.

After that nothing was normal anymore and Elsa dated all the turmoil and ultimate tragedy in her family from that evening of upheaval. She remained resentful of Zuzie the rest of her life without realizing why or that none of it was really Zuzie's fault.

On his way to school the next day, Paul took the folders back to Elsa's office and told them she would be on maternity leave for the next three months. That night he got the crib out of the basement and put it together.

Chapter 8

Elsa was dressed, preparing to leave the hospital. She put her purse on the bed and opened it to get her makeup bag. There was a folded report on top. Oh, yes, that case of the father who molested his baby girl. She'd forgotten all about it but she would have Paul drop it by the office so someone could follow up on it. She laid it on the white sheet of the hospital bed and never gave it another thought. She put on some lipstick and a dusting of blush. The orderly came with a wheelchair; it was silly but hospital rules forced her to use it to get to the car. Then Paul came in and a nurse brought the baby.

Elsa's homecoming with the baby was lovely. Paul had gotten the boxes of baby clothes out of the hall closet. The house only had four bedrooms so when Fern had volunteered to share her room with the baby early in the pregnancy, Elsa and Paul had been very relieved that there wouldn't have to be a battle over forcing Zuzie to share her room with her sister. Fern cleared out some dresser drawers and washed the baby clothes and folded them away.

Paul put the crib in Fern's room and the bassinette in the family room. Fern washed the frilly bassinette liner and flannel receiving blankets and got it all ready for occupancy.

Paulie retrieved the tub of baby toys, the ones that had survived three kids, and washed the plastic ones. He put the tub in the family room and went back to his video games, happy in the knowledge that he'd more than done his share. Even Zuzie pitched in and did some bed-making and vacuuming.

Paul went directly from school to the hospital and picked up his wife and new baby son. Elsa was holding the baby when they came through the front door. Paulie was the first to greet them, shouting for his sisters to hurry up and come see the new baby. All three children were entranced.

Elsa sat in Paul's recliner and the kids clustered around to see. Paul videotaped it all. The baby slept unconcernedly, perhaps knowing that he was safe in the bosom of his family.

Paulie slipped his finger against the baby's palm and the tiny fingers gripped it.

"Look," Paulie exulted. "The baby's got my finger. Boy, he's pretty strong for such a little guy."

"Look at his hair," Zuzie said. "It's so thick.

He's even got little sideburns."

"He's beautiful, Mom," said Fern. "Look, Dad, he's so sweet. Can I hold him?"

"After while," Elsa said. "When he wakes up."

"I want to hold him, too," Paulie piped up.

"Sure," Paul told him. He looked around at his brood and smiled happily. "Of course. You can all hold him after he wakes up. But you'll have to be very careful. He's not a toy or a rag doll, you can't handle him too much."

"Right, Dad," Zuzie agreed wearily. "I'm so sure we would mistake a baby brother for a toy."

"What did you name him?" Paulie wanted to know.

Elsa glanced up at Paul and smiled. "Samuel Timothy," she said. "After both his grandfathers.

"Oh, no, not Sam," Paulie groaned.

"Why not Sam?" Fern demanded. "Sammy's a beautiful name."

Zuzie rolled her eyes. "Like Dr. Seuss? Get it, Dimwit? *Sam I Am*?"

"All right," Elsa said in her stop this nonsense tone. "That's enough. His name is Samuel Timothy and that's final."

"That's right," Paul added. "You are not going to quarrel over your brother's name."

Zuzie laughed. "No matter how dorky it is. I mean, after all, you named me Zuzie."

"There's nothing wrong with Zuzie for a

name," Elsa said.

"No, not with the *name*," Paulie put in.

Paul decided to head off the sibling squabbling. "Come on, kids, help me get dinner ready. Let your mom and Sam rest a little."

He herded them out to the kitchen, Fern trailing after the others, reluctant to leave the baby.

Sammy was a happy baby. He throve in the atmosphere of love and care that his older siblings created and if they spoiled him a little, it was certainly understandable. Fern was especially attentive, and after Elsa went back to work, it was Fern who usually took care of Sammy in the interval between after school and her mother's return from work. She would go by the daycare center and pick him up, wheeling him home in the stroller, and playing with him until one of her parents got home. He was six months old when the graffiti started at school.

One day thick black ink in one of the boys' restrooms proclaimed: ZUZIE IS A WHORE.

One of the janitors, a man named Elvin Dravadowski, tried to scrub the words off the wall but had to paint over them. He reported it to the principal, Mr. Willis, who made a note of it.

Mr. Willis reflected that it had been awhile since the last outbreak of such graffiti. There was always some, of course, popping up all over the school, but such specificity was not so usual. He knew Zuzie Mills slightly and had thought her a fairly good student with a good family background. He hadn't expected her name to appear in such a context. Still, it didn't necessarily mean anything. High school boys didn't know much about whores, not, he reflected, that principals and teachers probably knew much about them, either. But to an adult a whore would be a professional while to a boy a whore was more likely to be "easy." Mr. Willis sighed. He asked his secretary to bring him a list of Zuzie's classes; he would talk to her teachers and the coaches, see if any of them had heard anything.

A few days later, FOR A GOOD TIME CALL ZUZIE MILLS 555-6689, was written in big black letters on the wall of the boys' locker room. The graffiti got uglier, nastier, and more frequent. Mr. Willis was upset. Elsa and Paul were angry. Zuzie was hysterical.

"I'm not going back to school," she cried one evening. "Everyone thinks I'm a whore and the boys are treating me like one. I'm not going back."

Elsa and Paul had sent Fern and Paulie upstairs to do their homework so they could talk to Zuzie and, hopefully, get to the bottom of the problem.

"You can't just drop out of school, honey," Paul said. "You won't solve anything by running away from your problems."

"You don't know what it's like. My friends look at me funny, like they believe the stuff on the walls. And the real whores have started acting all friendly and that just makes the boys believe it more. Today that Carl Mercer asked me to go out with him tomorrow night."

"What's so bad about that?" Elsa inquired. "He seems like a nice guy."

"Mom! He's not a nice guy. He all but raped Sandy. He's only got one thing on his mind. I'm not going to go out with Carl Mercer."

"You're not going to drop out of school, either," Elsa decreed. "Your father and I will go in and talk to Mr. Willis."

"What good's that gonna do? You already talked to him nine times. He can't do anything about it."

"Zuzie," Paul began, putting his arm around her, "don't exaggerate..."

Zuzie pulled away sharply. "Don't touch me. You don't care. My life is ruined and all you can say is, 'Zuzie, don't exaggerate.' I hate you!"

Zuzie ran upstairs and slammed the door to her room. Feeling that it didn't do justice to her rage, she opened it and slammed it again. She kept slamming it until Sam began to cry and Fern and Paul came out to see what was wrong with her.

"Stop it, Zuzie," said Fern. "You're upsetting

Sam. He can't sleep if you keep slamming doors."

"Yeah," Paulie chimed in, "I can't do my homework with all this door-slamming, either."

"That's right, it's all about you," Zuzie raged. "It's all about Sam. Nothing about me. You don't care what I'm going through. All you care about is yourselves. Fuck you." She went to the stairs and leaned over the banisters to shout down at her parents. "Hear that? I said 'fuck you.' Fuck you both. Fuck this whole family. I hate you all!"

Zuzie ran into her room and slammed the door one final time. She was too angry to sit still or read or even watch her little TV. She picked up her phone and called her best friend. Darla would understand. Darla was the one person left in the world she could talk to. Darla answered on the second ring and Zuzie poured it all out – her unfeeling family, her false friends, the principal and teachers who did nothing to help her.

The next morning, the first thing Zuzie saw when she walked into the school was a group of kids and a couple of teachers clustered at the intersection of the two main hallways, near the big double front doors. Her way to her locker went right past them so she set her teeth and tried to ignore them as she went by. But the teachers were so embarrassed and some of the kids were so interested in her that she unwillingly slowed down and looked at them. One of the boys laughed.

"Hey, Zuzie," another boy called, "what are you doing Friday night?"

"Not what," one of the girls giggled, "who?"

Miss Streatham tried to shush them but they were having too much fun.

"Do me next." Mark Pierce put his arm around her, letting his hand casually cup her breast.

Zuzie wrenched herself out of his embrace and Miss Streatham twittered ineffectually.

A couple of the girls grabbed a long streamer of butcher paper from one of the teachers and unfurled it so Zuzie saw it. In bright red letters a foot high it screamed, "Zuzie Mills fucks good." There was a crude, in every sense of the word, drawing to go with it.

"How about it, Zuzie," Alison Drury asked, "do you fuck good?"

Mr. Huerta grabbed the paper and wadded it up, telling the kids to go on about their business. Boys and girls both ignored him, joining in to taunt Zuzie.

Zuzie dropped her backpack and knocked Alison to the floor. Alison tried to fight back but Zuzie was too angry to even protect herself. She didn't even feel Alison's fingernails on her face. She connected with a hard, solid blow to Alison's mouth and kept flailing away with her fists.

"Get some help," Mr. Huerta said to Miss Streatham. "Get Mr. Dillingsworth."

Only too glad to get away from the melee, Miss Streatham fled down the hall, calling urgently for the vice principal. Mr. Huerta tried to break up the fight, without perceptible effect.

The noise and excitement attracted a lot of attention and there was a sizeable crowd pressed around the two girls when Mr. Dillingsworth arrived. He was a big, muscular man and in addition to being a vice principal, he was assistant coach of the varsity wrestling team. He didn't even pause to identify the combatants but immediately lifted Zuzie off Alison and set her on her feet. Alison was weeping copiously and the tears mixed with the blood from her mouth and nose made her look like a war zone casualty. Miss Streatham led her away, bound for the school nurse's office, crooning sympathy all the way.

Darla Welch pushed her way into the center of the crowd, having heard that Zuzie was fighting with Alison.

"Zuzie!" she screamed. "What happened? You're bleeding. Your face!"

Zuzie turned to her gratefully, clutching her arm. "Oh, Darla." She burst into tears and Darla started to lead her away, to get cleaned up in the girls' lavatory.

"Not so fast," Mr. Dillingsworth said, putting out a hand like a haunch of venison. "I need to talk to you, Miss Mills. In my office."

Zuzie was incredulous. Darla was indignant.

"Mr. Dillingsworth! Look at her," Darla exclaimed. "She needs to get cleaned up."

He saw the logic in that. "Ten minutes." He looked around at the rest of the students. "Okay, the show's over. Go to your classes. Go on, unless you want some detention time to think things over."

The kids scattered, chattering excitedly. They hadn't had so much fun in school since some boys put the skunk in the home ec room.

"What on earth was all that about?" Dillingsworth asked Huerta as they turned to go.

Huerta picked up Zuzie's backpack and handed it to Dillingsworth. "Here, this is Zuzie's. What set them off? This." He held up the wadded paper. "Let's go to your office and I'll show you."

He smoothed out the paper on Dillingsworth's desk.

Chapter 9

Zuzie cried and cussed in the girls' lavatory and when she saw the long raw scrapes that Alison had clawed on her cheeks, she shrieked and redoubled both tears and rage. Darla dabbed at her cheeks with a wet paper towel and gradually Zuzie calmed down. The bell rang and the other girls left for their classes, casting curious looks at Zuzie and Darla.

"What started it?" Darla asked. "I thought you and Alison got along okay."

"So did I. I bet she's the one's been writing all that horrible stuff about me on the walls."

"In the boys' bathroom?"

"Why not? She could sneak in during class when there's no one there."

"Well, anyway, what about this morning?"

"Okay. I came to school just like always. My mom and dad are so clueless. They have no idea what it's like and they keep yammering about education and totally don't care what I'm going through. So this morning when I got here the hall was full of kids staring at a big sign. It said something horrible about me and there was a picture, too. So some boy smarted off and then some of the others said things...” Zuzie started to cry again.

“But, Zuzie, what about Mr. Huerta and Mr. Dillingsworth? Didn’t they do anything?”

“Sure. They did something.” Zuzie paused to blow her nose and catch her breath. She stopped crying and, with her back against the wall, slid to the floor. Darla sat beside her.

“Well, what did they do?”

“Mr. Huerta wadded up the sign. Miss Streatham was there, too.”

“I’m sure she was a lot of help.”

“Yeah, about what you’d expect. Stupid bitch.”

“Okay,” Darla said. “I begin to see a little bit. But why were you pounding Alison?”

“Because she asked me if it was true, what the sign said. I just suddenly lost it and all I wanted to do was make her quit smirking at me. I hate her. I hate them all. I hate the stupid teachers. What are they here for, anyway? Aren’t they supposed to teach us how to act? So why didn’t they make the boys quit saying those things to me?”

Darla sighed. Explaining teachers and their quirks was a bigger task than she was prepared to undertake. “I guess we’d better go to Mr.

Dillingsworth's office" she said. "He said ten minutes and I think it's been longer than that."

"I'm not going. I'm going home," Zuzie declared.

Darla frowned. "Yeah, I know. But you really better stop by Dillingsworth's office first. If you don't, you'll never get to tell your side of it."

"I don't care. He's not going to listen to me anyway."

Darla nodded. "Probably not. You'll have to get your folks to help you straighten it out."

"That's a laugh. My folks don't give a damn about me. It's all Fern and Paulie and Sammy. Right now, Sammy's the only one that counts."

Darla stood up and pulled Zuzie to her feet. "You still have to see Dillingsworth. Come on and get it over with."

"You'll come with me, won't you?"

"Sure. Where's your backpack?"

"I don't know."

The two girls went to the vice principal's office. He looked at his watch and told them to sit down.

"Okay, Zuzie" he said, "let's hear it. Why did you attack Alison Drury this morning?"

"She started it."

"I've already talked with Mr. Huerta and Miss Streatham, so try to stick as closely to the facts as you can, please."

Zuzie shot a look at Darla. She took a deep breath and said, "Did they tell you about that sign?"

Dillingsworth picked up the butcher paper, now folded neatly, and opened it out on his desk. "This. Yes. It's nasty."

"That's all you've got to say? It's nasty?"

Dillingsworth folded it up and set it on the desk in front of him. "Tell me why you attacked Alison."

"I didn't. She..."

Dillingsworth cut in. "Zuzie, there were two teachers there and both of them say that you suddenly flew at Alison and started hitting her. All I want you to tell me is why."

"Because she was being mean to me."

"Mean to you. Mean how?"

Zuzie nodded at the folded sign. "She asked me if what it said was true."

Dillingsworth leaned back in his swivel chair and tried not to look amused. "That's all?" He leaned forward, intent now on making a serious impression. "For a few heedless words you viciously attacked her? Do you realize that she's probably going to have a black eye and you may have broken her nose?"

Zuzie burst into noisy sobs. Darla was furious.

"Mr. Dillingsworth, look at Zuzie. Alison did that to her. And that's not all, the..."

Dillingsworth interrupted. “That’s enough, Darla. Zuzie, be quiet and listen to me. Whatever anyone said to you, you reacted with violence and that’s bad. Be quiet!”

Zuzie was far from quieting down. Fifteen minutes later, time that seemed much longer to Dillingsworth, she was still sobbing. He called the school nurse and tried to send Darla to class.

“I’m staying with Zuzie,” she defied him. “Someone’s got to stick up for her.”

Mrs. Andolfo, the nurse, came and led Zuzie to her office. Alison was lying on the cot, waiting for her mother to come and pick her up. When she saw Zuzie, she sat up, displaying a mixture of apprehension and bravado. She was holding a cold pack to her face and cotton rolls protruded from her nostrils. Zuzie laughed through her tears. That laugh was too much for Alison. She scrambled off the cot and grabbed Zuzie by the hair.

“Whore!” Alison screamed. “Bitch-faced whore!”

Zuzie lowered her head and rammed her shoulder into Alison’s chest, throwing her off balance. Both girls fell against the wall in the narrow room and Alison let go of Zuzie’s hair, trying to break her fall. Neither of them knew anything about fighting or they might have done some serious damage. As it was they managed to inflict some bruises on one another and Alison's nose resumed bleeding when the cotton rolls fell out. They made enough noise for half a dozen cat fights, what with crying and calling each other names. Mrs. Andolfo tried to get them apart but only got in the line of fire, collecting a few bruises of her own. Darla ran for help. She didn't want to get Dillingsworth but didn't know who else to go to when she saw the head janitor, Mr. Dravadowski coming down the hall. She ran to him.

"Come quick," she said. "The nurse's office. They're fighting."

Dravadowski took off on a lope, saw the situation in the nurse's office, and waded in. He grabbed Alison around the waist and pulled her away. Zuzie made a lunge for her but Mrs. Andolfo caught her. Darla stood in the doorway, thinking that if her best friend had been in deep doo-doo before, she was now truly up Shit Crick without a paddle.

"Darla," gasped Mrs. Andolfo, "go get Mr. Dillingsworth."

Darla went.

Dillingsworth was mad. What on earth had possessed Mrs. Andolfo to take Zuzie to her office while Alison was still there? Now here was more trouble for him to sort out and try to deal with. He eyed Zuzie balefully. Her lip was swollen and bleeding, her face was streaked with blood and tears, and her hair was an absolute mess. Alison was even worse. Blood was running from her nose and her eye was beginning to show some bruising. Mrs. Andolfo was fussing over her, trying to get her to sit down so she could stanch the bleeding.

"All right, Zuzie," Dillingsworth said. "My office."

Darla snatched up a tissue and began to dab at Zuzie's lip. Zuzie flinched and took the tissue from her, holding it to her split lip.

"Now." Dillingsworth said, in the tone that brooks no argument.

Zuzie and Darla started down the hall, Dillingsworth right behind them.

"Darla," he said, "you may go to your class. Zuzie is the one I need to talk to."

Darla shot him a defiant glare. "I'm coming with her."

The two girls sat in the visitors' chairs facing Dillingsworth's desk while he sat behind it. He looked at them in silence for a few moments.

"Okay, Zuzie, suppose you tell me what this is all about. I realize that you were upset this morning but I want to hear you justify this violent behavior."

"She called me names."

"You must be familiar with 'sticks and stones

may break my bones but names will never hurt me.' It's practically the first thing kids learn when they start school."

"Yeah. I've seen Coach Harrison when someone's dad gets on his case at a football game. He got thrown off the field once for going up in the grandstand to sock someone."

"We are not here to discuss Coach Harrison, Zuzie, we're here to figure out what to do with you."

"I don't care what you do to me. I'm not coming back here anyway."

Dillingsworth sighed. "We'll have to get your parents in for a conference. What's your mother's phone number? And your dad's?"

"Why should I tell you? You're just going to call them and make more trouble for me."

"Believe it or not, I'm not the trouble-maker in this scenario. I can get the phone numbers from your file, you know."

"Fine, do that."

"Zuzie, you are not doing yourself any good with this attitude. You've got to straighten up and cooperate."

"Why? You don't care anything about me. About what happens to me. All you care about is darling Alison." Zuzie's voice rose and she began to cry again. "Sweet little Alison got a black eye and a bloody nose. Poor Alison."

“Zuzie! Calm down. Stop yelling.”

“No!” Zuzie was screaming now. “I won’t stop yelling. I’m sick and tired of everyone blaming me for everything. No one cares about me, it’s always me that gets in trouble for everything. I’m not the one started all this shit. I’ve been persecuted for weeks and you don’t care anything about my feelings. You don’t even try to find out who is doing this to me. All you care about is your stupid school. That’s all my mom and dad care about, too. They don’t care about me. ‘Just ignore it, Zuzie,’ that’s what they say. Oh, sure, Dad pretends to care. He gets all lovey-dovey and puts his arm around me. I told him not to touch me. If he doesn’t care enough to help me, I don’t care about him. And mom won’t do anything about it. She just pretends she doesn’t see anything wrong and picks Sam up. I hate them and I hate this school. I wish it would burn down.”

Darla was trying to calm her friend but Zuzie was past listening to anything much less listening to reason. She jumped to her feet, picked up a small brass football from the desk – one of Dillingsworth’s most treasured possessions – and threw it at him. Darla was aghast, fearing that lightning might very well strike Zuzie dead. The football struck Dillingsworth on the cheek.

There was a new janitor that term. A young

heavyset woman. She was cleaning the glass on the trophy case just outside Mr. Dillingsworth's office. She could hear Zuzie very clearly and took note of what she screamed. She thought she could make use of it. Rhonda Thwait smiled as Zuzie burst through the door and down the hall to the big outer doors.

Chapter 10

Rhonda had barely managed to hang onto her hope that she and Virge could get their babies back from the state. All the Children's Services people would tell them was that the children were safe and being well cared for. The lawyer had told them that it would be possible to get Logan and Griffin back but it would be an expensive undertaking and might take a couple of years. They talked about it on the way home from his office one afternoon in late May. The children had been taken in January.

"We'll have to sell the house, that's all," Virge said.

"We don't really have much equity in it. Maybe we could take out a second mortgage," Rhonda suggested.

"Maybe. The thing is, we have to look like a stable marriage in a secure financial situation or the Children's Services people will recommend against us."

"I know." Rhonda slumped in her seat,

depressed, with a hollow feeling in her stomach and an ache in her heart. “Virge?” She was afraid of his reaction but she had to bring it up.

“Yeah?”

“You need to ease off on your drinking. They won’t look favorably on us if they think you’re an alcoholic.”

He jammed his foot down on the accelerator and began to weave in and out of the freeway traffic, slamming on the brakes when he couldn’t see an opening. “That’s right, it’s my fault. Nothing is ever your fault, it’s always me. Let me tell you a few home truths, Rhonda. If you hadn’t insisted on getting your fat slob of a sister to babysit, none of this would have happened.”

“Virge, I didn’t mean that it’s your fault,” Rhonda cried, tears brimming.

“Oh, here we go with the waterworks! Give it a rest.”

“I’m sorry. If you only knew how sorry I am.”

“Yeah, I’m sorry, too. Sorry I ever got tangled up with you. Have you looked at yourself lately? You’re as fat as Karen.”

Rhonda didn’t even try to defend herself. She cried harder. Virge took the next exit and pulled to a stop in front of the first tavern he saw, “Magruder’s Sports Bar.” He gave Rhonda a look of loathing and went inside. Rhonda waited for nearly an hour before her temper flared. Thinking of the terrible things Virge had said to her, she got her keys out of her purse and drove to the drug store. He would be furious when he came out and the car was gone but she didn't care. Serve him right.

Things went from bad to worse after that. Virge became very erratic about going to work and his drinking spiraled out of control. First they lost the house, then the store, and Virge's car was repossessed. Rhonda rented a small apartment but Virge didn't move with her, he took refuge with his parents for a couple of weeks and then disappeared from Rhonda's life. None of the Thwaits would tell her where he was and she wasn't really sure that they knew. She took a job with a temp agency and got enough work to pay her rent and buy her groceries.

The idea of getting even with Elsa Mills grew in Rhonda's mind. At first she had tried to contrive ways to kill her and not be caught. Then it occurred to her that it would be much more satisfactory to exact revenge. Retribution, really. An eye for an eye, a tooth for a tooth. As Elsa Mills had injured her, she would injure Elsa Mills. She set to work to find out everything she could about her enemy. It was surprisingly easy. After the house was gone and with it the computer and most of the furniture, she discovered that the public library had computers available for patrons and began to do her research there.

Mills was an unfortunately common name but she knew the address and phone number of the state office where Elsa worked. A brief bio posted on the site had given her the husband's name and the fact that she had three children and their names. She wasn't sure if the baby had been stillborn or if the bio hadn't been updated. She found Zuzie Mills' blog, which seemed to have new postings every day or two. The new baby's name was there and a whole lot of useful information in previous posts. Zuzie really poured out her heart in her blog. It wasn't long before Rhonda had all the information she needed. She quit her temp agency and got a job as janitor at Zuzie's school.

She was a little sorry to put Zuzie through hell but reflected that you can't make an omelet without breaking eggs. Zuzie was a good girl, a little selfish and lazy, but not more so than most of the kids. It had surprised Rhonda how easy it was to ruin the girl's reputation. She had seen the change in the way the other kids treated her and also in the way the teachers treated her. No one, least of all the teachers, doubted for a moment that the scribblings on the boys' lavatory walls were true. No one made any effort to find out who was responsible for the graffiti or if there might be some ulterior motive behind it. That made Rhonda angry. When she saw Dillingsworth with his cheek swollen and a rich purple in color, she took a certain pride in her handiwork. It served him right. It looked very painful.

She was cleaning the woodwork in the hall outside Dillingsworth's door when Elsa and Paul Mills came in. She gave them a long, steady look but neither of them more than glanced at her. She had put on so much weight that Elsa wouldn't have recognized her anyway but Rhonda saw that Elsa was the type who never bothered looking at menials. She resolved that she would peel some of that arrogance away before she was through.

Dillingsworth closed the door after ushering the Mills into his office. Rhonda had hoped to hear their conversation but there would be other opportunities. She was still working on the woodwork when the door opened and Dillingsworth and the Mills came out.

"Oh, just a minute," Dillingsworth said. "Zuzie's backpack. She forgot it yesterday and I didn't notice it until she'd gone. She left it in the hall so I brought it in here."

"Thanks," Paul Mills said. He slung it over one shoulder and shook hands with Dillingsworth.

Rhonda smiled to herself, congratulating herself on her foresight in taking the birth control pills out of Ms. Edlemann's purse when the opportunity presented itself. She had thought she might be able to use them sometime and sure enough, she had. Seeing Zuzie's backpack in Dillingsworth's office when she went in that afternoon to empty his wastebasket, she had tucked the pills, minus the pharmacy label, in one of the pockets. There were only a few pills left so Zuzie's parents would think she'd been using them right along.

That night, as Rhonda wrote checks to pay her utility bills, the thought popped into her mind that teachers are very vulnerable in certain ways. She finished as quickly as she could in order to think about that vulnerability. In the present climate of willingness to let government officials circumvent safeguards to personal liberty in the name of safety, Rhonda knew that if she could plant even a modicum of suspicion of Paul Mills, she could pretty much ruin his life. School authorities were strangely unwilling to investigate teachers but she thought parents could be fairly easily goaded into demanding action against him. She decided to go to the library that night and send a few email messages. She would send one from the school's computer lab, too.

Two mornings later Joe Clutterbuck, the principal of the middle school where Paul Mills taught, opened his email to find a message from "petetorres638" at a hotmail address. The subject line said, "Re: Paul Mills." The message informed him that Mr. Mills was sexually abusing his daughter Zuzie and advising him to ask Darla Welch because she knew all about it. Clutterbuck was dismayed. He didn't believe it. Paul Mills was the most sane and well-adjusted man of his acquaintance. Besides, he and his wife had just had a baby. Some malicious fool was throwing stones at random, hoping to stir up trouble. He decided not to play into it.

Over at the high school Principal Willis and Dillingsworth both received a message from petetorres638. Theirs was cruder: "Zuzie Mills dad is fucking her. Isn't that against the law? Ask Darla Welch what she knows about it." The messages were sent separately, however, so neither knew of the other's. Willis decided to ignore it; Dillingsworth decided to have a man-to-man talk with Paul Mills. On second thought he'd better talk to Darla first. He looked up her class schedule. She had algebra first thing, then English. He glanced at his watch. The bell would ring in about ten minutes.

Mr. Dillingsworth pulled Zuzie's record up on his computer. Her grades were good, nothing spectacular like straight A's but a solid B average. Until this term. Algebra, biology, and American history were bad, barely passing. English was a little better but she was flunking French. Even P.E. was only a C. He'd have to talk to her teachers, see if they knew anything about this sudden downturn. The bell rang and he went to find Darla Welch.

Darla was apprehensive but defiant. She sat in his office, glaring at him, clearly expecting the worst.

"Come on, Darla," Dillingsworth said. "If Zuzie's having some kind of problem, I need to know about it so we can get her some help."

"I was here yesterday, remember? I saw what kind of help you're giving her."

"You know Zuzie very well, don't you?"

"We've been best friends since fourth grade."

"So you've been to her house a lot, I guess. Doing homework, slumber parties, just hanging out."

Darla eyed him suspiciously.

"Please answer me, Darla."

"Well, what's the question?"

"You aren't going to do anyone any good with that attitude. Do you spend time at Zuzie's house?"

"Yes, of course. And she spends time at mine. Why?"

"How does she get along with her family? She has siblings, doesn't she?"

"She has a sister and two brothers. She gets along with them just fine. Sometimes they squabble but it's not a big deal."

"How about with her parents? Does she get along with them, too?"

"Well, sure. They get on her nerves sometimes. Everyone's parents get on their nerves sometimes. I'll bet your parents get on your nerves, too."

Dillingsworth scowled at her. "Get on her nerves how? What do they do that irritates her?"

"Listen, ask them. I'm not going to gossip about the Mills."

"I'm serious, Darla. There's nothing gossipy about this. I need to know how Zuzie gets along with her family. She's changed from a quiet, normal, good student to a hysterical screamer whose grades have taken a nosedive. I need to know why so I can figure out how to help her get back on track."

"She's tried to tell you. You and the teachers. She's been telling you for weeks and you just ignore her. Like yesterday."

"Did it really look to you like we were ignoring her yesterday? I thought she did quite well making herself the center of attention."

Darla shook her head. "See, that's what I mean. You totally ignored Zuzie's problems and took Alison's side. Alison started it, not Zuzie. But you came down on Zuzie and acted like the whole thing was her fault."

"Let that go for a minute, will you? Tell me

about Zuzie and her parents. Did she ever say anything made you think she was really angry with them? Not just irritated but really mad."

"Yes. She's been mad at them because they blame her for making trouble at school and it isn't her fault but they won't listen."

"Try to remember some of her actual words when she told you about some of these incidents."

"I don't remember her actual words. I'm not a tape recorder."

"Well, does she seem mad at both her parents or just one? Maybe her mom. A lot of teenage girls go through a phase of being mad at their mothers."

"Sure, I know that. No, she seems madder at her dad." Darla became thoughtful. "I don't know why. They used to be pretty close."

Dillingsworth nodded. "Fathers and daughters are usually close. When they're little, girls want to marry daddy when they grow up."

Darla shot him a look of contempt. "Well, Zuzie doesn't want to marry her daddy. The other day she didn't even want him to hug her."

"I don't see how you could possibly know that."

"She told me so."

"Just like that. Walked up to you and said, 'I don't want my dad to hug me.'"

"No, of course not. We were talking on the

phone. She had just had a big fight with her folks and she was upset. She said something about him wanting to be all lovey-dovey but she'd told him to keep his hands off her."

"Really? Sounds like she's really mad at him."

"That's what I've been trying to tell you."

"I understand that Zuzie is a very angry young woman but I don't know why."

Darla shook her head, casting her eyes heavenward. "Because you won't listen."

"I'm listening now."

"All right." Darla leaned forward, eager to explain her friend's problem to someone who was willing to help her. "Someone has been writing nasty things about Zuzie on the walls of the boys' bathroom. You saw that banner thing yesterday. Everyone is treating her differently this term. Of course she's upset."

"That's when you first noticed the difference in Zuzie? The beginning of this term?"

"Yes. When the graffiti started."

"What else is different this term?

Chapter 11

Elsa went back to work when her maternity leave was up and found her in-box piled high with all sorts of papers. Some of the cases she had been working on were still pending but some had been finalized. She sorted them into various piles and decided to skim through the final dispensations first. Eventually she came to the Thwait file. The name rang no bell in her memory so she began to read documents. There was a lab report. A diaper had been found to contain fecal matter containing lamb, rice, beets, and milk. No human blood was present. Memory hit her with an almost physical force. The little girl had not been molested. Her father was innocent. And she, Elsa Mills, had taken the children away from their parents. Suddenly, she felt nauseous. Her hands shook as she flipped through the file, looking to see what had been done.

There it was, the court order: the children were to be returned to their parents forthwith. Elsa relaxed, drew a steadying deep breath. It was all right after all. When had they gone home? More papers. Another report from another investigator. The Thwaits had moved. They were no longer owners of record of their little pharmacy. The investigator hadn't been able to locate them. Another court order, this time to let them be adopted as abandoned minor children. That was all. The actual adoption papers would be in someone else's files in another department of the bureau. There was nothing Elsa could do. She told herself that firmly, very firmly. Gradually the times became more infrequent when her mind presented her with a contradiction, informing her that she could do something and should do something. She steadfastly suppressed all such thoughts and she very carefully told no one anything about the Thwait case.

It was Saturday afternoon and Fern was playing with Sammy in the family room. He was such a delightful baby, cheerful and content, always ready to smile. At eight months he could sit up by himself and crawl and Fern was fascinated. He had begun to pull himself up and stand, holding onto the furniture and looking around for applause at his cleverness. Fern always obliged, telling him what an extraordinary child he was.

Elsa came into the room carrying Zuzie's

backpack. She set it on the coffee table and plopped down on the couch. She unzipped the main compartment and began taking books and papers out.

Fern looked at her apprehensively. It seemed that for the past few weeks every time her mother even thought about Zuzie, yelling was the result.

Paulie came wandering in, wearing his baseball mitt and tossing a ball back and forth.

Elsa glanced up. "Don't throw the ball in the house, Paulie."

"I'm not, Mom."

Elsa sighed. "Paulie."

"Well, I'm not, I'm tossing it. Tossing is not the same as throwing."

"Whatever you call it, don't do it in the house. You know better."

Paulie dropped the ball and mitt and went out to the kitchen. He came back a minute later crunching an apple.

"What are you doing, Mom?" he asked. "That's Zuzie's backpack. She'll be mad if she sees you going through it."

The back door opened and they could hear Paul and Zuzie. For once they were laughing together. Fern relaxed. Things had been so bad lately that she'd tensed up just knowing that Zuzie was in the house. Maybe today would be pleasant for a change. They heard the refrigerator door open and shut and Paul and Zuzie came in, each popping the top of a can of soda.

"Guess what, Mom," Zuzie began. She stopped dead and stared at her mother.

Paul's shoulders slumped, foreseeing another screaming match. Just when things were so much better. He very badly wanted to turn around and go back out the door. He didn't, of course, because he was a good husband and father. He went to sit beside his wife on the sofa.

"That's my backpack. You have no right to search it." Zuzie was trying to stay calm.

"Oh, yes, I do. You are a minor child and I am responsible for you. You have no rights except those I grant you." Elsa didn't even look up; she went on removing things from the backpack.

"Honey," Paul said. "I don't know if that's the best approach here."

"I do. Zuzie, I'm going to get to the bottom of this and you're going to straighten your act up."

"Get to the bottom of what, Mom?"

"Of why you have suddenly gone off the rails like this."

"Gone off the rails? That's what you call it when I'm being persecuted? I've gone off the rails?"

"No one is persecuting you. That's just plain silly." Elsa looked up at her eldest child. She had always done her best to bring the kids up right.

Because she loved them but also because with her job, it wouldn't look too good if her own kids got into trouble.

"It's not silly, it's true," Zuzie's grip on her emotions was slipping and Paul could see that an outburst was imminent.

"Let's back up a minute, here. Elsa, could you stop for a minute so we can talk this over calmly?"

But just then Elsa unzipped one of the small compartments and found the birth control pills.

"I see," Elsa said, coldly calm. She stood up. "Yes, I see just exactly how persecuted you are. Zuzie, how long have you been taking these pills?"

"I don't even know what they are, Mom."

"Please don't insult my intelligence. I want to know where you got these pills and how long you've been taking them."

Zuzie snatched the pills out of her mother's hand and Elsa slapped her. Paul stepped between them. Zuzie whirled and ran up the stairs. Halfway up she stopped and turned. She screamed her rage and frustration at them and hurled her open soda at her mother. Luckily, it missed, but hit the coffee table, and sprayed sugary brown syrup all over the room and everyone in it. They all hollered at once and Sammy began to cry. Zuzie's door slammed. Elsa started to go after her but Paul grabbed her arm.

"No." He glanced at Paulie, who was staring at them while Fern picked Sammy up tried to quiet him, dabbing at him with a handful of tissues. She looked up and saw her dad's expression.

"Come on, Paulie," Fern said. "Mom and Dad need to talk."

"Well, I'm not stopping them," Paulie replied.

"Oh, come on," Fern said with weary patience. "I'll play you a game of 'Vengeance Raiders.'"

"All right," he agreed, "only let's play 'Terran Paleolepidoptera.'"

"Okay. Get it set up while I clean Sammy up."

The kids went upstairs and Elsa turned to Paul furiously. "How dare you? How dare you interfere when I'm disciplining one of the kids?"

"I'm sorry, honey, I just don't think that's the way to handle this."

"Obviously."

Elsa went into the kitchen. She picked up a roll of paper towels and a spray bottle of cleaner. She took them into the family room and began to clean up the soda. Paul took some paper towels and began to blot soda out of the carpet.

"Listen," he said, "Zuzie is having a rough time. The graffiti, the fight with Alison, the mess with Mr. Dillingsworth."

"Again, obviously. And thanks to her, we're having a rough time. I can't believe you're taking her side."

"I'm not exactly taking her side," Paul said. "I'm trying to find out how to help her. Something's very wrong here and we need to get to the bottom of it. I don't think screaming and slapping are the best way to do it."

"What's wrong is your daughter has turned into a tart and I won't have it. She's taking birth control pills and God knows how long she's been taking them. Or where she gets them. She's probably taking other kinds of pills, too, maybe smoking marijuana. If you won't do anything about it, I will."

"Elsa, please, listen to yourself. A young girl does not suddenly do a complete turn-around without some kind of trauma triggering it. We need to find out what's wrong before we start throwing accusations around. This is just going to make matters worse."

"So now it's my fault! You have always favored Zuzie and spoiled her by giving her everything she wants. Well, you're not going to shield her from the consequences this time. She has danced the dance and now it's time to pay the piper."

"You don't even know what's going on with her. Let's speak with her calmly and try to see her side of whatever this is."

Elsa stared at him. "What's wrong with you?

Your daughter is having sex with who knows how many boys and you want to find out what's going on? She gets in fights at school – did you see Alison? Did you see the damage your daughter did? Did you see the vice principal's face? She nearly broke his jaw. She did loosen two teeth. The girl is completely out of control."

"Something's wrong with her."

Elsa laughed unpleasantly. "You got that right."

"Well, instead of convicting her without a trial, why don't you try talking to her to find out what it is?"

"I don't know where you and Zuzie got the idea that this is a courtroom. This is my home and I'm going to run it as such."

"I, I, I. You talk like you're the only one who counts. Like your word is law."

"Maybe it is. You are such a wimp. You always have been."

Paul nodded. "I always know when you have lost the argument because you start calling me a wimp."

"I have not lost this argument. In fact, I have never lost an argument with you. You are incapable of winning an argument. You are too soft, too wishy-washy."

Paul went past her toward the back door, his car keys in his hand.

"And now you're leaving. If you're so macho, why don't you stay and fight it out?"

"If there was any hope that you would be reasonable, I would. But you are nothing more than an overdeveloped ego, devoid of intellect and incapable of rational thought."

He opened the door and she screamed after him, "Don't you dare leave this house. I am not through with you. Don't you dare walk away from me."

"You are really pathetic, Elsa."

Paul went out the door and as he started to pull it shut behind him, Elsa hurled the spray bottle at him. It caught him just behind the left ear. She was frightened for an instant but it was not heavy enough to do any serious damage. He stopped momentarily, then went on out without looking back at her.

Chapter 12

Rhonda Thwait sat at her kitchen table listening to a tape over and over. Frustrated at not being able to hear the vice principal's conference with Paul and Elsa Mills, she had bought a voice-activated tape recorder. It was not as big as a pack of cigarettes so it was easy to hide. She had used duct tape to fasten it under the seat of his desk chair. She had felt a little foolish as she carefully wiped her fingerprints off both recorder and tape roll and used plastic gloves as she worked. There was virtually no chance that fingerprints would come into play even if the recorder was discovered but there was no sense in taking chances. Not until she was finished with her project. After that she didn't care what happened to her.

The tape wasn't very good quality and she could only make out part of the actual words used. But it was enough. There were lots of irrelevant noises and conversations on both phone and in person that were of no interest. But the conversation between Dillingsworth and Darla Welch was pure gold. She would send a couple more emails the next day – keep the pot boiling.

The next night Rhonda had a new tape to listen to. She smiled as the school counselor and the vice principal discussed Zuzie Mills and her problems. She knew the counselor's name was Delbert Cunningham.

Dillingsworth: "Come on in, Del. Have a seat."

Cunningham: "What's up, Carl?"

Dillingsworth: "It's this mess with Zuzie Mills. You've talked to her, haven't you?"

Cunningham: "No. By the time I heard anything about it, she was refusing to come to school. I tried to make an appointment with her parents but so far no luck. What's going on with that family, anyway?"

Dillingsworth: "Well, let's see what you think. First her grades started to slip a little, then they took a real nosedive. She's always been a solid B student, now she's getting D's and even failing a couple of classes."

Cunningham: "I heard there's been some nasty graffiti in the boys' lavatories."

Dillingsworth: "Yeah. The usual garbage. [laughter] Did you hear about the banner the other day?"

Cunningham: [laughter] "Yeah, Huerta was

talking about it and about the cat fight between Zuzie and Alison Drury."

Dillingsworth: "She punched Alison out all right."

Cunningham: "Why Alison? Did she accuse Alison of making the banner?"

Dillingsworth: "I don't know. By the time I got there, they were rolling around on the floor and Alison was a bloody mess. Luckily, Zuzie doesn't know anything about boxing."

Cunningham: "She knows a little about throwing, looks like. Your jaw is still a little swollen and the bruising hasn't quite faded out."

Dillingsworth: "The little bitch. Threw that brass football at me. Knocked two teeth loose and damn near broke my jaw."

Cunningham: "What did you say that got her so riled up? These girls aren't usually violent. Not to that extent."

Dillingsworth: "I don't really know what set her off. She was talking about the graffiti and I was trying to get her to talk about what she'd done to Alison."

Cunningham: "That's odd. That she would react so strongly. Hers isn't the only name on the bathroom wall."

Dillingsworth: "True. But it's the most surprising one."

Cunningham: "Why do you say that?"

Dillingsworth: “Her mother works for Children’s Services and her father is a teacher over at Roosevelt Middle. Zuzie doesn’t wear the makeup and clothes that most of those girls wear. She doesn’t fit the profile.”

Cunningham: “She doesn’t fit your idea of the profile. What’s going on at home? You’re no doubt familiar with the adage about minister’s sons being the wildest kids in town.”

Dillingsworth: “I had her parents in here the other day. They’re nice people. Nothing out of the ordinary seems to be going on with them. They have two younger kids and a new baby. No obvious signs of excessive stress or problems.”

Cunningham: “A new baby. How new?”

Dillingsworth: “I don’t know. I think they said he’s six months old or so.”

Cunningham: “So he was born around the time Zuzie started being a problem student?”

Dillingsworth: “I guess. Roughly speaking.”

Cunningham: “How old is Mills?”

Dillingsworth: “I’d say around forty. A year or two either way.”

Cunningham: “You know what this adds up to, don’t you?”

[Pause.]

Cunningham: “You do know what it sounds like, right?”

Dillingsworth: “Oh, hell, Del.”

Cunningham: “It’s not unusual for a man to break out at that age. His wife’s pregnant and his teenage daughter is right there.”

Dillingsworth: “Come on, he’s a nice guy.”

Cunningham: “Yeah, so was Ted Bundy.”

Dillingsworth: “This is nothing like that. Paul Mills is no killer.”

Cunningham: “Probably not. All I’m saying is being a nice guy does not preclude a man from also being a bad guy. In fact, sometimes a nice guy represses all those nasty urges until some day he loses control.”

Dillingsworth: “And it’s not unusual for a sexually abused young girl to turn sexually promiscuous.”

Cunningham: “You got it. Looks like a textbook case.”

Dillingsworth: “You know what this means.”

Cunningham: “It’ll have to be reported to Children’s Services. They’ll investigate and if they find evidence, they’ll inform the D.A.”

Dillingsworth: “This is going to ruin the poor bastard’s career, you know. Even if he’s innocent.”

Cunningham: “I don’t see what else we can do. The law is very clear. It has to be reported.”

Dillingsworth: “All right, I’ll talk to Mr. Willis.”

Cunningham: “Right. It’s the principal’s

responsibility."

There was a little more hemming and hawing but as soon as she was sure that's what it was, Rhonda turned the tape off. She sat and thought about the conversation she had just heard and how she could use it. This was going to be good. Once the school authorities suspected, there was nothing on God's green earth that could save Paul Mills. He could deny it until hell froze over and no one would listen. Even Zuzie could deny it without even making them think twice. Victims often suppress abuse, relegating it so deeply in the unconscious that they actually had no memory of it. Elsa Mills was a trained professional and the pattern was so classic that she would believe it automatically, with no evidence, even of her own husband.

Rhonda smiled. There was nothing more that she needed to do. Any further emails would only look suspicious now. She could sit back and watch as the Mills family was torn apart. It promised to be better than reality TV.

Chapter 13

"What?" Paul was stunned. "You're out of your mind."

Principal Clutterbuck sighed. "I'm sorry as hell but you know the rules, Paul. The accusation has been made. I've got to put you on administrative leave until we get it cleared up. I want you to know that I have every confidence in your innocence. I don't believe for one second that you abused Zuzie or anyone else."

"Who says I did? Who made the accusation?"

"You know I can't tell you that. Children's Services will carry out an investigation. What happens next depends on what they find."

"How long will it take? How long am I going to be on leave?"

"I don't know. It's out of my hands, Paul. Go get anything you need from your desk and your locker."

Paul stared at Clutterbuck for a long moment then got up and left the room. It was lunchtime so the classroom and locker room were empty when he got his briefcase and a few personal items from his desk and then picked up his sweats and other stuff. He tossed it all in the back seat of the mini van and drove numbly out of the parking lot. When he pulled into the driveway at home, he stopped and sat slumped behind the wheel for a few minutes. He restarted the van and backed out. He needed someone to talk to but there didn't seem to be anyone. No one but Elsa. She would be home in four or five hours. He would drive around awhile.

Paul found that he was too miserable to drive. He stopped at the lake in one of the city parks and sat on a bench, staring out at the water. People were all around him. Joggers, dog walkers, grandparents or maybe great-grandparents pushing strollers with babies in them. People were intent on their own lives, neither knowing nor caring that his own life was imploding. Slowly, anger built in him. From feeling numb, confused, and flattened, he began to feel angry and belligerent. But he was still confused. He wanted to confront someone, have it out with them, find out why they had leveled this terrible charge at him. He knew himself to be normal, sane, mentally healthy. He had no sexual urges that couldn't be satisfied with his wife. What could possibly have made someone think otherwise?

As he sat there and thought about it, the

conviction grew that no one could think otherwise. No one who knew him even slightly could think he was sexually abusive to teenage girls, especially not to his own daughter. That meant that someone was maliciously accusing him, solely in order to cause him trouble. To embarrass him. Even send him to jail. But that was just as incredible as the accusation. There couldn't be anyone who hated him enough to do that. He was aware that not everyone he encountered liked him; he knew a couple of guys who detested him. But they weren't his enemies. They wouldn't set him up for this kind of trouble.

The more he thought about it, the more he thought that was the only answer. Someone did hate him, did want him to be run through the meat grinder of an investigation. From anger, he moved into fear. There was nothing to find. There could be no evidence because he had done nothing wrong. A conviction would cost him his job, would send him to jail. It would cost him his family, too, probably. He had no illusions about Elsa's reaction. She would divorce him and he would not get even joint custody of his kids. Hell, she would make sure that he was denied any access to them.

He told himself to calm down. This was unnecessary because he was innocent. None of it would happen because there was no evidence and there would not even be a trial. Elsa knew he was a good father. There was nothing to worry about. Just cooperate with the investigation so it would be over quickly and he could get his life back to normal.

The first hint that it wasn't going to be that simple came when he got home and saw Elsa's face as he told her about it. There was no warmth in it, no sympathy. He was shocked. Surely, she didn't believe he'd done what he was accused of.

"No, of course not," she said. "I know you're a good father. You would never molest any child, much less your own."

Paul felt there was something she wasn't saying. They were in their bedroom, Elsa sitting cross-legged on the bed, Paul on the vanity bench facing her.

"But what?"

"What do you mean? But what?"

"I don't know," he said, slowly, thinking, trying to gauge her feelings. "I guess I feel that there is a 'but' in what you just said. You believe in me, but."

"There is no 'but,' it's just that I'm in rather a peculiar position here. My job is to protect children."

Paul nodded. "And it looks odd, to say the least, to have your husband accused of abusing a child."

Elsa was relieved. She hadn't known what to expect, whether Paul would be so stunned that he couldn't see her point of view or what. So it was a relief to see that he did understand that there would be repercussions to her.

"Well, it does. I'm trained to observe and recognize the signs. It makes me look incompetent if such a thing could go on in my own home without seeing it."

"Clutterbuck wouldn't tell me anything, naturally. Who made the accusation or what they said."

"Naturally. That would be confidential information. But I'm wondering what whoever it was saw or heard that made them turn you in."

"Turn me in? That sounds like..."

Elsa waved it away. "Evidence. That's what I mean. There can't be any evidence because you didn't do it but there has to have been something someone saw or heard or thinks he saw or heard to make him suspicious."

"What happens now? Who investigates and how do they go about it?"

"Someone from Children's Services will talk to people who know you and Zuzie. They'll talk to Zuzie, too, and to you. They won't find anything and that's what they'll report."

"And then I can go back to work and we can forget all this hoo-ha?"

Elsa frowned. “It won’t be quite that simple. After the final report is made, you’ll be put on the list of people to monitor for a year or so. Eventually, when there’s no sign of deviance, you’ll be taken off the list.”

“But I’ll be able to go back to work?”

“I don’t know, Paul. Sometimes the report recommends that the person under investigation not be in a position where he or she has access to children. Just as a precaution.”

Paul was distressed. “You mean even when the report clears me, I might not be able to go back to teaching? Where’s the justice in that?”

Elsa looked out the window at the gathering dusk. “Well, you have to look at it from the professional’s point of view. Just because they don’t find anything doesn’t necessarily mean there’s nothing to be found. How many times has an investigation cleared someone only to have him victimize other children? Think about the headlines – MAN CLEARED BY INVESTIGATORS KILLS TWO-YEAR-OLD. No agency wants to see headlines like that so we try to err on the side of caution.”

“Elsa, we are not talking about an anonymous perpetrator here, we’re talking about your husband, who happens to be innocent.”

“I know, honey. I’m sorry you have to go through this. I’m just trying to be realistic.” She looked at him, then, and the distance in her eyes stabbed through him.

He took a moment to fend off the pain then said, "What are we going to tell the kids?"

"Oh, lord, I don't know. I think we'd better tell them the truth. They'll hear it from their friends. Better they hear it from us first."

That went better than they expected. Paulie was confident that his dad would be vindicated and everything would be all right in a day or two. Fern realized that it was very serious but had no way to gauge the chances it would be quickly and positively resolved. Zuzie immediately connected it to the campaign against her. For that one evening, the Mills family stood together. Paul told the kids that the investigation would not find anything wrong and he would soon be back at school. Then he suggested they play the "Game of Life." They all gathered around the kitchen table, even Elsa, and had a good time, all together. They took turns holding Sammy, who laughed and bounced and kept reaching for the game pieces. It was the first time they had done anything as a family in weeks. It was the last time ever.

Two days later, Zuzie and Fern were in the family room with their parents when Paulie brought the mail in. He handed it to Elsa. She flipped through it and opened one with the Roosevelt Middle School return address. It was the official letter from Clutterbuck, telling Paul he'd been placed on administrative leave while allegations of the sexual abuse of his daughter were being investigated, Elsa read it and handed it to Paul. He read it and dropped it on the coffee table. Zuzie snatched it up and read it.

"See!" she exclaimed. "See! It's all part of the lies people have been telling about me at school. Now maybe you'll believe me."

Elsa closed her eyes and shook her head.

"Oh, I don't think so, honey," Paul began. He stopped abruptly.

"See," Zuzie said triumphantly. "You do think so. It all fits together."

"Zuzie," Elsa said, "don't be ridiculous. Fern, where's Sam?"

"He's asleep, Mom," Fern answered.

"Did you give him his supper first?"

"I fed him at five, just like always. Why?"

"Don't take that tone with me, young lady."

Fern got to her feet and went out to the kitchen.

"Come back here, Fern. Right now," Elsa called.

Fern came to the door of the family room. "What?"

"I don't know what's the matter with this family. You girls are both getting so rude and hateful, I swear I hate to come home," Elsa said.

Zuzie looked at her mother incredulously. "What planet do you inhabit, Mom? You think you hate to come home? If I could think of one single other place to go, I wouldn't stay here one more minute."

"Oh, yes, poor Zuzie," Elsa mocked. "The weight of the world on your shoulders."

"Just stop it, Mom," Zuzie cried. "You make Fern do all your work here at home. You make her take total care of Sam while you sit on your ass and whine about how hard you work at the office."

"That's enough. If you weren't out of control, out doing God knows what – although those pills make it pretty plain – with God knows who, maybe you could pitch in a little here. And now that your father is out of work, maybe you'll acknowledge that it's a good thing I do have a job."

Paulie started to cry quietly and went up the stairs. He looked back once to see if anyone noticed him. Paul was looking at him but made no sign to him.

"You are such a bitch!" Zuzie screamed. "I hate you!"

Zuzie ran out the door, pausing in the kitchen to grab her mother's keys off the counter. Paul ran after her but wasn't quick enough. They heard the car start and Fern and Elsa ran out the back door.

“I’ll try to head her off,” Paul said, wrenching open the door of the van as he fumbled in his pocket for his keys.

“Oh, my God,” Elsa yelled. “She has no license, not even a learner’s permit. I doubt if the insurance would even cover it if she wrecks the car.”

Fern shot her mother a look of disgust and went inside. She fixed a couple of sandwiches and poured two glasses of milk.

“What are you doing?” Elsa asked.

“Fixing something for Paulie and me for supper.”

“Oh, just for the two of you? Nothing for me?”

Fern gave her mother a direct eye-to-eye look. “You’re okay,” she said, picking up the food and starting up the stairs.

Chapter 14

Paul was grimly following Zuzie. Between her emotional upset and lack of experience, she had several very close calls. He pulled up beside her a couple of times and honked, motioning for her to pull over but she only gunned the accelerator and he was afraid she would wreck so he backed off and just followed her. When she pulled onto the freeway ramp, he figured she was going to her grandmother's, which was probably the best they could expect from this escapade.

Dolores Chastain was Elsa's mother and she and Zuzie had always been especially close, even though Elsa was not especially close to her mother. She had been widowed a few years earlier and had decided to stay in the old family home. It was a friendly house, spacious and comfortable and just a little shabby. It had been built in the early 1920s and had a broad front porch and a miniscule free-standing garage. Huge old shade trees gave the neighborhood an air of gracious dignity.

When Zuzie turned into the driveway, bumping one front tire over the curb, Paul parked on the street. He had decided to give her a little time with her grandma before joining them. Zuzie ran from the car to the house, slamming the front door and locking it behind her.

"Grammy! Grammy, where are you?" Zuzie yelled.

"Great Scot, Zuzie, what on earth is the matter?"

Dolores peered around the high back of her chair and, seeing and hearing Zuzie in an apparent panic, scrambled to her feet. She wrapped her arms around the girl and held her. Zuzie burst into tears. Dolores saw Paul through the big front window and wondered why he didn't come in, too. Then she saw Elsa's car in the driveway but no one in it. Puzzled, she drew Zuzie over to the sofa and sat down with her, keeping one arm around her.

"Shhhhhh. It's all right, Zuzie. You're okay, now. Tell Grammy about it. What is it that's upset you so?"

Zuzie gradually quieted. "Oh, Grammy, it's been horrible."

"It must have been. Now, go and wash your face, love, while I make us some tea. Then I want to hear all about whatever this is. I'll call your dad in and we'll have a nice chat."

"No! No, please, Grammy, don't call him in. Please don't."

Dolores didn't want her to start crying again. "All right, honey, I won't just yet. Go ahead now and I'll make the tea."

"Promise you won't call him in while I'm gone."

"I promise. My goodness, it must be some brouhaha."

Zuzie sniffled and went upstairs to the bathroom. Dolores went to the kitchen and filled the teapot from the instant boiling water tap, dropping tea bags in it. She put it on the table in the breakfast nook and set the cookie jar and two mugs beside it.

Zuzie came down the stairs and into the kitchen. She set a box of tissues on the table, foreseeing that she would probably need them before she got her story told.

Dolores poured the tea and watched Zuzie over the rim of her mug. Zuzie took a sip and smiled at her grandmother.

"Grammy, can I stay here with you for a while?"

"If it's okay with your mom and dad. We'll have to figure out what to do about school."

"Mom and Dad won't care. They'll be glad to get rid of me."

"Oh, honey, don't say that. They love you very

much. You know they do."

"Well, maybe Dad does. But Mom doesn't. I think Mom hates me." Zuzie started crying again.

"Zuzie, honey, I know you've been having a hard time at school but don't make things worse. Your mother loves you and only wants what's best for you. Now, tell me why you are so upset."

Zuzie nodded and concentrated on stopping her tears and controlling herself so she could speak. She sipped her tea and stared down into the liquid. Tears still trickled down her face but she was doing her best to be calm.

"Grammy, did Mom tell you about Daddy?"

"That he'd been suspended or put on administrative leave or whatever they call it? Yes. Some nonsense about molesting you. I don't believe it for a moment."

"Mom does. Oh, she doesn't come right out and say so but you can see it in her face when she looks at either of us. And she freaks out when she sees us together."

"But, that can't be right. You must be mistaken, honey."

"No, I'm not. I heard her talking to Lily on the phone." Zuzie smiled rather shame-facedly at her grandmother. "I know I shouldn't have eavesdropped but she was talking about me."

Dolores smiled. "I suppose I should scold you but I just want to know what she said."

"Well, she said she didn't believe that Daddy would abuse any child, especially not his own daughter. Then she told Lily that she'd talked to me – she did, too, and it was so embarrassing. Plus, it made me mad that she would even ask, much less act like she was the D.A. or something. Anyway, she told Lily that I had denied it but that didn't mean anything because abuse victims often had hysterical memory loss when they were attacked by someone close to them. And she talked about the graffiti at school and said it wasn't unusual for victims of sexual abuse – that's how she described her own daughter: victim of sexual abuse – to be promiscuous. And how I denied that, too, even after she found the birth control pills in my backpack."

Zuzie choked up and then began to sob again. Dolores set her jaw in anger at what these enlightened people were doing to her granddaughter. Zuzie always spent weeks with her in the summer and she knew Zuzie well, better than either of her parents, because she listened when Zuzie conversed with her. The profile that fit many abuse victims did not fit Zuzie. Elsa should be able to sort this out.

Dolores reached across the table and took Zuzie's hand. Zuzie squeezed Dolores' hand, but not too hard on account of her grandmother's arthritis.

"I guess it's not surprising that your mother is taking this attitude. After all, she sees so much of the abuse and neglect and their effects."

"I don't care," Zuzie exclaimed. "She ought to know me better and she ought to give me the benefit of the doubt. What about due process? What about the rules of evidence? What about impartial investigation? She hasn't done anything but jump to conclusions."

Dolores was very troubled. She had never expected problems of this magnitude in her family. She had little experience with such things and felt completely bewildered. But she was a strong woman and she had always coped. She would cope now.

"I know you are feeling betrayed, honey, and it must be hell for you."

"Yes, it is." Zuzie felt a bit better, finding her grandmother supportive and sympathetic. "I really am still a virgin, Grammy. I don't know who put the pills in my backpack."

"I believe you. I can't imagine who would do such a thing but I believe that they are not yours. Could it be a nasty prank? Maybe one of the girls at school wanted to get you into trouble for some reason?"

"I don't know. Maybe. Or one of the boys. I don't know why anyone would want to get me in trouble, though. But I don't know why anyone would keep writing those horrible things about me on the bathroom walls, either. It's so bizarre, Grammy!"

Dolores nodded. "It is that." She glanced out the window at the car in her driveway. "When did you get your driver's license? I thought you weren't going to get it until your next birthday."

Zuzie flicked a look at the car. "That's right. Mom thinks I'm not mature enough yet. She won't even let me get my learner's permit."

Dolores just looked at her.

"Okay!" Zuzie burst out. "I took Mom's car without her permission. I guess I stole it. But I had to get out of there. I couldn't stand it one more minute. You should have heard the awful things she was saying. I hate her!"

"Oh, now, Zuzie, don't talk like that. Let's stay as calm as we can. Your mother is going to be pretty angry about the car."

"I know. I'm surprised she hasn't been on the phone to you before this, telling you to bring me right straight home."

Dolores nodded. "I expect she will be soon. Okay, honey, I think we'd better get your dad in here and talk it over with him."

"I'll go get him," Zuzie offered. She took a couple of tissues to mop up with and went out the back door.

Chapter 15

Paul was sitting in his car, watching the house for any sign of welcome. He sat up straighter when he saw Zuzie coming toward him. He opened the door and got out, searching her face for any sign of her feelings. She smiled at him.

"Come on in, Dad. Grammy's a nice, sensible person. She believes us both."

Zuzie gave her father a hug and he returned it, nearly in tears himself from strain and relief. They went to the back door hand-in-hand. Dolores opened the door and gave her son-in-law a hug.

"Come in, Paul. Come in and let's talk."

She had made a fresh pot of tea and poured them each a mug. Paul stirred a spoonful of sugar into his.

"How are the other kids? Sammy's thriving, I take it?"

"They're fine," Paul said. "The baby is growing by leaps and bounds. You'll have to come see us before he gets so big you won't recognize him."

"From what Zuzie says, I need to come see you and give my daughter a good spanking."

"Don't do that, Grammy, you'll get arrested for child abuse."

Dolores shook her head. "This whole thing is simply incredible. Someone evidently hates the whole Mills family."

"It almost seems like a vendetta," Paul said. "But I've racked my brains and I can't think of anyone I've injured or even ticked off to such an extent. I mean, it would take an awful lot of time and effort. Who would care that much?"

"I don't know but it's either that or an astounding series of coincidences."

Zuzie chimed in. "What are the statistical odds of getting this by coincidence?"

"Astronomical, I agree," Paul said. "But I just can't make it make sense that someone is deliberately framing us both."

"I don't think we can get anything constructive done from that angle. There's nothing to go on, nowhere to start." Dolores shook her head.

"There sure isn't," Paul agreed.

"Then what are we going to do?" Zuzie demanded.

"We've got to think what's best for the family," Dolores said. "Now, maybe I shouldn't say this but I'm going to, anyway. In my opinion, Elsa isn't handling Zuzie's problems very well. I don't know how you feel, Paul, but I know my granddaughter. She is not promiscuous and she hasn't been sexually abused. Not by you, not by anyone else."

"I don't think so, either," Paul said. "In spite of the pills. I don't know how they got in your backpack, Zuzie, but I do not believe they were yours."

Zuzie's tears started flowing again and she dabbed at her eyes with tissues. "Thanks, Dad. I don't know how they got there, either, but they aren't mine. I never saw them before. I didn't even know they were birth control pills until Mom said so."

Dolores patted her hand. "It's going to be all right, Zuzie." She looked at Paul. "I don't see any sense in Zuzie going back to school there. She can't study in all that turmoil and there's no reason to subject her to the emotional trauma." Dolores grinned at Zuzie. "I'm sure it was satisfying, momentarily at least, to smack that girl, but beating people up isn't really going to solve anything."

"We've been considering boarding school." Paul divided an apologetic glance between the two women.

"I won't go." Zuzie stated. "I want to stay with Grammy and go to school here."

"Zuzie," Paul said, "I don't think it's fair to

ask your grandma to take responsibility for you. If it weren't for that, it would be the best answer, at least for now."

"Nonsense, Paul," Dolores said. "I think it's the only sensible thing to do at this point."

"Please, Daddy. I'll be good and help with the housework. I won't give Grammy a hard time. Please let me stay here."

"I don't know what your mother will say," Paul said. "Or rather, I do know. I've been talking to her on my cell while I was waiting out in the car."

Dolores and Zuzie waited for him to continue. He reached into the cookie jar and took a couple of homemade cookies.

"Spice cookies!" exclaimed Zuzie. "My favorite." She reached in and took a handful.

Paul tilted the jar toward Dolores. "No, thanks," she said.

"Well," Dolores prompted. "What did Elsa have to say?"

Paul chewed cooky and swallowed. "About what you'd expect," he said. "Or what I'd expect, anyway. I am to bring Zuzie home instantly or she will call the cops and swear out a warrant."

"What did you say, Dad?"

"Nothing that helped much, I'm afraid. But we do have to go home."

"I'm not going home," Zuzie stated. "I'm

going to stay here with Grammy."

"You'll have to go and get some clothes, Zuzie," Dolores told her. "And your schoolbooks and things."

Zuzie shot a look at her father. Paul nodded.

"Okay," Zuzie said. "Okay, I'll go. But just long enough to get my stuff. Then I'm coming back here."

"All right," Paul agreed.

"Promise, Dad. You have to promise."

Paul hesitated. "I promise. But understand, Zuzie, I'm only promising you can come back here tonight for a little while. I'm not promising that it will be permanent."

"Okay, I'll settle for that," Zuzie said with a grin.

"I'll get my purse," Dolores said.

She left the kitchen and Paul took out his cell phone and punched in his home number.

"It's me, Elsa," he said into the mouthpiece. "Dolores is going to drive your car home and we'll talk the whole thing over."

Zuzie watched him anxiously, her cooky forgotten in her hand.

"There's no point in hashing it over on the phone, we'll be there in twenty minutes or so."

Zuzie made a face at her dad and he frowned at her.

"All right, you do what you have to do. Only I

would appreciate it if you would wait a few minutes until we get there. This is not just your problem, Elsa, this is a family matter."

Paul listened a moment, then said, "See you in a few." He snapped his phone off and put it back in his jacket pocket.

Dolores came into the room carrying her purse. "Well," she said, "let's go find out what Elsa's got to say."

Chapter 16

Rhonda was restless. She was doing fine in her plan to destroy Elsa Mills' family but she had no access to Elsa. She wanted to see the woman writhe in pain and fear. She wanted to know that Elsa was suffering, not just think she must be. But how to get to her? That was the problem. Rhonda picked up her purse. She would go to the library. Maybe she could get an idea there. A book or maybe something on the Internet.

If Rhonda could have seen how much hurt she was inflicting on the rest of the Mills family, she might not have cared to go on with her campaign. But she didn't know and as long as she didn't see it, she didn't really care. The only thing of importance to her was causing pain to Elsa Mills in the same way Elsa had destroyed her.

The library was only a few blocks from Rhonda's apartment. She walked to it and nodded with a pleasant smile at the librarian she met just inside. It was her policy to do nothing to make herself memorable, either by being unpleasant or unduly friendly. She found a vacant computer station and sat down. She had brought a small notebook and pen and took them out of her purse.

As a Children's Services employee, Elsa should be vulnerable to accusations of abuse, just as her husband was. It would look pretty bad to her boss if she could be shown to be abusive. Not to her own kids. Rumors of sexual abuse were not nearly as easy to use against women as men. This called for something different. Rhonda ran several scenarios through her mind. Physical abuse of children in her custody? Emotional abuse of her own children? Spousal abuse? What about parents or grandparents? Did Elsa have responsibility for anyone in those categories?

Money. Maybe instead of abuse of people she could be framed for abusing her trust in some way that concerned money. What funds would she have access to? The trouble was, Rhonda thought, she didn't really know enough about Elsa's job or her personal life. She went to the Children's Services website and punched up the "about us" page again. It didn't look as if Elsa would have access to any funds she could steal. Rhonda toyed with the idea of making her look like a sneak thief, which appealed to her sense of humor, but she would have to get a job as a janitor or something in Elsa's office to make that work and she didn't want to change jobs. Not yet, anyway.

Anonymous letters. Could she manage to send anonymous letters and make Elsa look like the one who sent them? Rhonda thought about it. That might work. She could make Elsa look irrational to the point of mental instability. That ought to cost her the job at Children's Services. What kind of letters and to whom? Rhonda exited the program and the library to go home and think about it.

When Marvin Sorenson opened the anonymous letter, he was surprised. Not at receiving an anonymous letter – Children's Services received scores of them and as director, he was very familiar with them. But he could not recall ever receiving one at home before. This one was computer generated, laser printed. There was nothing unusual about the paper or the envelope.

> ARE YOU SURE YOU KNOW ALL OF YOUR WIFE'S MEN FRIENDS? IS ALL OF HER TIME ACCOUNTED FOR?

Such tripe. About Jolene, of all people. Simply the last woman in the world to have an affair. Marvin tore the letter into pieces and threw it in the wastebasket. There was another one in his office mail the next day. His secretary brought it to him as he was sitting at his desk, trying to figure out how to justify some of the items on the proposed budget for next year.

"Mr. Sorenson, this came in the mail and I didn't think I should just leave it in your in basket."

"What is it, LaTishia?"

He glanced up at her and took the letter she handed him. The envelope was clipped to it.

> YOUR WIFE HAS BEEN SEEN IN A CERTAIN MAN'S CAR UNDER QUESTIONABLE CIRCUMSTANCES. AREN'T YOU CURIOUS?

"It wasn't marked "personal" or anything," LaTishia said. "I wouldn't have opened it, if it had been."

"No, it's all right," Marvin reassured her. "I mean, it's all right that you opened it. I'm sorry you had to see it. I have evidently made someone angry; this isn't the first one I've gotten.

It turned out it wasn't the first one received in the office. A couple of days later Sandy Benson, who was the personnel director, knocked on the door jamb, the door standing open. Marvin looked up from the intractable budget.

"Come in, Sandy. Have a seat. What's on your mind?"

Sandy seated herself and handed him a small sheaf of documents. He glanced at them and then gave them a longer look.

"We've got a problem," she said.

"So I see. These were not all sent to you?"

"No. A couple of people brought them to me but I have reason to think that several others have received similar letters."

Marvin read a couple of them.

DO YOU REALLY APPROVE OF YOUR SON DOING DRUGS? ASK HIM WHERE HE WAS LAST SATURDAY NIGHT AND WHY HE HANGS OUT WITH THAT DRUG PUSHER.

YOU ARE ALWAYS BRAGGING ABOUT HOW CLOSE YOU AND YOUR HUSBAND ARE. HE WAS PRETTY CLOSE TO THAT BIG BLOND FROM THE STATE PLANNING OFFICE THE OTHER NIGHT WHEN YOU WERE WORKING LATE. MAYBE YOU SHOULDN'T LEAVE HIM UNSUPERVISED SO OFTEN.

He looked back at Sandy. "Yeah, I've gotten a couple myself."

"Sometimes," Sandy said with a wry smile, "I long for the old days when we had typewriters that didn't try to do our thinking for us and didn't offer idiotic suggestions about our grammar. Then I remember carbon paper and spell-checker. The point is, with typewriters you had a little something to go on with anonymous letters. They were idiosyncratic enough that you could identify which machine a letter was typed on and sometimes you could identify the typist by the way some letters were darker than the others. Or lighter."

Marvin nodded. "Whereas, with computers, none of that applies."

"Right. All we've got to go on is the paper and that would take an expert. It's all pretty much alike to me."

"Me, too."

"Still, we need to do something about this. It's gone beyond the mere nuisance level. We've got people snarling at one another, accusing each other of being the poison pen."

"And it's only a matter of time before someone gets one that hits home," Marvin said. "God only knows what would happen then."

"We've got to find out who's sending them."

Marvin examined the envelopes. "Postmarks aren't any help."

"No, the post office sends everything for miles around to that big regional office to cancel the stamps."

"Do you think they're the work of someone here in the office?"

Sandy nodded. "I think so, yes. Quite a few people must have grudges against the agency, or think they have cause to, but they aren't the kind of people who would think of writing anonymous letters. They'd be more likely to spray paint graffiti on the building."

"Besides which," Marvin said, "people like that don't usually spell all that well. Or use words like 'unsupervised.'"

"The writer is obviously unbalanced but educated."

"Well, I don't quite see where we're going to go from here with this."

Sandy hesitated. "You don't think we need help?"

"You mean, call the cops?"

Sandy nodded. "There must be detectives trained to deal with anonymous letter writers."

Marvin was doubtful. "It would be totally undesirable to have the police poking around this office. It would look as if we don't trust our own people."

"Not necessarily."

"We are not going to call the police in. Maybe I should speak to the staff."

"And say what? I don't know, Marvin, I don't think that's what we need here."

"Tell me what you think we need, then."

"Let's just give it a few days and see what develops. Maybe the miscreant will give himself away. Or herself. Anyone that disturbed shouldn't be that hard to spot."

"All right. I'll give it a couple days. Bring me any letters you get hold of and see what you can find out about anyone under more stress than usual."

"You got it." Sandy stood up and stood for a moment, looking at the anonymous letters on Marvin's desk. She shook her head. "I thought I knew my people. I would have said no one on our staff would stoop to anonymous letter writing."

She sighed and left the room.

Rhonda had no way of knowing how well her letters were doing in the Children's Services office. She was normally a patient woman but as she saw her project nearing its end, she was eager to take the final step that would finish her quarry. After three weeks, she decided to wrap up the anonymous letter campaign.

One evening she took a few minutes in the computer lab at the high school and printed a few letters from her flash disk. On one of them she printed on the back, in the same font:

> PROBLEM WITH PAUL AND ZUZIE IS DRIVING ME CRAZY. CAN YOU THINK OF

That would give whoever got the letter enough information to identify Elsa Mills without being so crude as to actually name her. Rhonda smiled as she put the flash disk back in her pocket and put the letters in a file folder. She took the folder to her locker and put them in her purse, then went back to work, cleaning the corridors with a wide, oiled dust mop.

LaTishia handed Marvin Sorenson his mail. "You got another of those letters," she said.

"So I see," Marvin answered. "Hold my calls until I give the word, would you LaTishia?"

"Okay."

As soon as the door closed behind LaTishia, Marvin picked up the phone and called Sandy Benson.

"Sandy? Can you come to my office, please?" Then, "Yes, now, if it's convenient. Bring any anonymous letters you have."

Sandy tapped on the door and entered without waiting for permission. "What's up?" she asked, sitting in one of the visitors' chairs. "Another letter?"

Marvin nodded. "A different twist this time."

He handed it to her and she noticed the printing on the back, as she handed him a couple of letters she'd managed to get hold of. She read the message on his:

DOESN'T IT BOTHER YOU THAT YOUR FINANCE

OFFICER IS FEATHERING HIS NEST WITH AGENCY MONEY? OR ARE YOU IN IT WITH HIM?

"Nasty but harmless, there being no defalcations." Sandy opined. "Did you see this on the back?"

"No. What's it say?"

Sandy handed it back to him. "I think that pretty well tells who "Anonymous" is."

Marvin read it and said nothing for a moment. "Elsa Mills? She seems an unlikely anonymous letter writer."

"I don't know who would be a likely one in this office. But "Zuzie" is a pretty unusual name and I do know that Elsa has been under a great deal of stress the last few months. It might have pushed her over the edge, psychologically speaking."

"Aside from her new baby, I'm not aware of anything stressful in her life. What's going on with her?" Marvin, as with most CEOs, was not in the loop of office gossip except at the senior staff level.

"The new baby is eight months old," Sandy said. "She's been having a bad time with her daughter. Zuzie's sixteen and seems to have gone off the rails somewhat. I don't know exactly what's wrong, booze or drugs or sex or what, but Elsa's been upset about it for quite a while. And her husband lost his job."

"Elsa's husband? He's a teacher, isn't he?"

Sandy nodded. "Eighth grade. What I heard is that he's suspected of some kind of sexual misconduct. Naturally, Elsa hasn't said much about it. That I've been able to find out, anyway."

"That's ugly. Especially for a teacher." Marvin sighed. "Okay. Let me think about this. If you hear anything relevant, be sure to let me know. Or if you get hold of any more of the letters."

"All right." Sandy stood up to go.

"And, Sandy, don't talk about any of this. It's a mess and it's going to get worse but we need to keep as much of it as we can to ourselves – just you and me. Okay?"

"Of course."

Chapter 17

A few days after Zuzie had gone home with her grandmother, Paul and Elsa had a bitter confrontation. It was precipitated when Elsa came home from work to find Paul and Fern sitting on the couch in the family room, laughing together. She frowned as she set her purse and briefcase down in the foyer and hung her coat up. She went into the family room and saw that neither Paulie nor the baby was there.

"Where's the baby?" Elsa asked, sitting on one of the chairs by the card table, where a jigsaw puzzle was about half finished.

"Hi, Mom. He's napping," Fern said, then turned back to her dad. "What happened after that, Daddy?"

"Where's Paulie?" Elsa asked.

"I let him go over to Umberto's house," Paul said. "Hard day, honey?"

"Yeah, it has been. Fern, your father and I need to talk."

Fern shot her mother an exasperated look.

"Okay, I'll go read a book or something." She went up the stairs and they heard her door close.

"Well, let's have it," Paul said. "I can see you've got something on your mind."

"I think it would be best if you move out for a while," Elsa said.

"I can't pretend to be surprised because I've kind of been expecting you to do this, but I wonder if you realize what it will mean for me and all of us."

"It'll mean that some of the pressure will be taken off me. It's sheer hell at work and no better here at home. I need some breathing space."

"As usual, it's all about you. Well, just exactly where do you suggest I go?"

"You could stay with you brother. Or one of your jock buddies."

"I suppose I could, for a while, but I'm not going to."

"Listen, Paul, there isn't any money for you to rent an apartment. You're going to have to swallow your pride and stay with Evert and Mona. If you stay here, it looks as if I condone what you've done."

Suddenly, all the pain and rage Paul had been controlling erupted. That he didn't even raise his voice impressed Elsa more than a tantrum would have.

"You've finally said it. You believe it's true.

You actually believe that I am not only capable of pedophilia but that I have molested my own daughter. I see you stiffen every time you see me near Fern. I see you wonder every time I put my arm around Paulie or hold Sam. I know you don't want me to touch you. Maybe you haven't noticed that I have no desire to touch you. There is no warmth in you, Elsa, not for me, not for the kids. I can't remember now what there might have been about you that ever appealed to me. But get this: I am not moving out of my home. I am not abandoning my children. If you want to leave, go. But the children stay here with me."

"You think it's all going to go your way? I don't think so. I think I hold the winning hand here. I'm not the one on administrative leave for sexual misconduct."

"Neither am I." Paul said. "I was anonymously accused. There's an investigation underway. Since there is no evidence, because I'm innocent, I will be exonerated. Then I'll go back to teaching."

"Mr. Clutterbuck wouldn't have put you on leave if he didn't have reason to suspect you."

"He had no reason but that anonymous letter. The same as those that people in your office have been getting. That your co-workers think you've been sending."

"They do not." Elsa's voice was getting louder with every sentence. "No one thinks I'm the poison pen." She jumped to her feet and began bouncing around the room.

Paul laughed. "Oh, yes, they do. You've never been any too well liked, you know. You're vain and arrogant and now that you're under all this stress, they think you've snapped and taken to anonymous letter writing."

"Who told you that? I never told you anything about those anonymous letters. How do you even know about them?"

"Unlike you, I have friends, Elsa. Friends who believe in me."

"Roy. Roy Tucker. That S.O.B. He's always hated me, I'll bet he's the one. Isn't he?"

"Give it up. What does it matter who told me? How about it? Did you write them?"

"You bastard! Shut up! Anyway, we're not talking about letters, we're talking about you getting out of this house. Now. Tonight."

"That's settled, Elsa. I'm not moving out. I'm going to move into Zuzie's room for the time being. This weekend, I'll start partitioning the garage to make myself a room and bath out there."

Elsa screamed, "No, you won't." She picked up Sam's roly poly clown and hurled it across the room. "You aren't going to stay here and live off me. You aren't bringing anything in to help with expenses and I'm not going to support the kids and you, too." She grabbed Fern's box of CDs and began to throw them. "All you do is sit around on your ass all day, working puzzles. I won't have it."

"You are really pathetic, you know that? Flouncing around the room, breaking the kids' toys and ruining Fern's CD collection. "I swear, you are less mature than any of the kids, even Sam."

Elsa picked up a brass vase from the fireplace mantel and threw it at him. It struck him on the shin.

"Get out! Get out! I can't stand the sight of you."

Paul stood up and went to her, limping slightly. He took her by the shoulders and forced her over to the mirror and held her so she had to look at herself.

"That's what you can't stand the sight of, Elsa. Look. Look at what you've become. How do you like what you see? A selfish, screeching, bitch. Attractive, isn't she?"

He let go of her and she whirled to face him, weeping noisily.

"I hate you. I hate you! Get out of my house and out of my life. Right now or I'll call the police and have you arrested."

"I don't think you want to do that. I really don't think you want to either call the police or threaten me with it. You're the violent one here. And I don't think it would look very good to the folks at Children's Services. You've already driven your daughter away from home and you've alienated all your co-workers. I think you'd better leave well enough alone. Or maybe I should say bad enough alone."

"You can't stay here. You can't. You don't even have a job." She continued to cry, sobbing and gasping.

"Oh, didn't I tell you? I do have a job. I start at Gary's Gym Monday. Teaching exercise classes and coaching a couple of the volleyball teams. Now, get yourself together so I can bring the kids down for dinner."

Paul went upstairs to move his clothes into Zuzie's room and explain the new arrangement to Fern. This last was unnecessary because Fern had heard almost all of it and was sitting on the floor holding her teddy bear with tears streaming down her face.

By the time Marvin Sorenson called Elsa into his office several days later, she was nearly hysterical. Paul had been right about her co-workers knowing about the anonymous letters. No one, of course, said anything directly to her. Nevertheless, she was well apprised of their feelings. Some refused to look at her unless she got right in their faces and more or less forced them to; some looked her right in the eye with cold disdain; others smirked and snickered and whispered.

“Sit down, Elsa.”

Elsa sat, eyeing Marvin apprehensively. Her conscience was clear as far as her work was concerned but she had an idea this wasn’t going to be about work. Not directly.

“How are you, Elsa?”

“Okay. How are you?”

“Fine. Just fine. Everything at home all right?”

“We have our ups and downs but we’re okay.”

“Baby doing well?”

“He’s fine. Listen, Marvin, what’s this all about?”

Marvin was acutely uncomfortable. “You seem to be more than usually stressed and the quality of your work isn’t up to your usual standard. I just wondered if you need to take a little time off. Or anything.”

“I am a little more stressed than usual but I wasn’t aware that my work was suffering. What, exactly, is your complaint?”

“You’re late with reports, for one thing...”

“Of course I’m late with reports! You pile on the work until it’s all I can do to see the clients, do the investigations. The only time I have for writing reports is in the evenings. I do have a life, you know. A husband and children. But if you want me to, I'll spend my family time writing reports." Elsa stood up. "Is that all?"

"Sit down, please. No, that isn't all."

Elsa sat again. She was nearly in tears.

"I wanted to talk to you about some anonymous letters that..."

"I am not the poison pen! I don't care what anyone says, I'm not the one who's writing the damn things. You have no right to accuse me of it. You have no evidence, just someone spreading rumors and lies."

"It was my intention to ask if you had received any," Marvin said calmly. He found Elsa's reaction very interesting. Almost a confession to interrupt him with a denial like that. "What makes you think someone is spreading the rumor that you wrote them?"

"The way everyone acts. They all hate me. I think whoever it is wrote them to try to get me into trouble."

Marvin leaned forward a little. "And why would anyone expend that much energy to get you into trouble?"

Elsa started to cry. "I told you. They hate me."

"Why should anyone hate you? That's pretty strong language for the workplace."

"I don't know why they do, they just do."

Marvin relaxed a bit. "You know, we often get

negative thoughts when we're under extraordinary stress. Sometimes it seems the whole world is out to get us."

Elsa swabbed her eyes with a tissue. "Yeah, I took Psych 101, too. Look, are we finished here? Because I've got work to do."

"Actually, we aren't quite finished, Elsa. When you said we didn't have any evidence, you were mistaken. We do actually have some."

Marvin took the letter with the "Zuzie and Paul" fragment on the back of it out of a desk drawer and handed it to her. She read the letter.

"So what? Another anonymous letter."

"Turn it over."

She did so. "This is your evidence? You think this proves that I wrote these damned letters? You think I would be stupid enough to use a piece of paper with this on it to print an anonymous letter on?"

She stood up, tore the letter into pieces, and threw it on his desk. He stood up, too, and glared at her angrily.

"If you think that destroys the evidence, you are very much mistaken. On the contrary, it gives it added weight."

"So you're going to do what? Fire me? You can't, I quit. I don't need the aggravation of this stupid job or all you stupid people." Elsa's voice rose with each phrase until she was screaming.

"You're a stupid jerk, anyway. Asshole!"

She turned and ran out of the room, nearly cannoning into LaTishia who was standing near the door with her eyes big.

"Get out of my way," snarled Elsa. "You stupid bitch."

Marvin followed Elsa to her desk and watched as she began to throw her belongings into her purse and tote bag. She glanced up and saw him there.

"What the hell are you doing, Marvin? Get away from me."

Marvin didn't move and Roy Tucker rolled his chair out into the aisle to see what was going on. Several other people peeked and peered around the cubicle walls to watch. Elsa looked around at them.

"Oh, I get it," she said. "You're escorting me from the building to see that I don't do anything to the files or anything. Fine." She raised her voice. "I hope you're all enjoying this! Little excitement to enliven your day. Take a good look because you won't be seeing me here anymore. You'll have to find someone else to take your spite out on. I hope she likes anonymous letters. You really should have been able to think of something more creative than that. But I don't care! You're all assholes anyway. You hear me? Assholes!"

She took her chair by the back and rammed it into Marvin as hard as she could, then began to throw the items on her desk – the stapler, the tape dispenser, the polished rock she used for a paperweight.

Marvin grappled with Elsa, trying to get her into her chair and away from throwing ammunition.

"Call Security," Marvin grated.

Roy rolled forward to his phone.

Chapter 18

It was early when Elsa got home after her brouhaha at the office. By the time the security people got to her, she had calmed enough that all they had to do was escort her to her car. She drove home in a white heat of fury but in control, outwardly calm. No one was there. She wasn't often alone in her home and it felt very strange. She left her things in the foyer, clamped her jaw, and got set to work her anger off. She'd start cleaning in the family room.

But there was nothing to do in the family room. It was neat, no toys or homework papers or snack dishes scattered around. The kitchen, then. But it, too, was clean and tidy. She walked through the house and found that every room was as it should be except Paulie's and hers. There were some dirty clothes on the floor of Paulie's room and some toys were strewn around. She picked up, putting the clothes in the hamper and the toys on shelves. She made her bed and cleaned her bathroom. There wasn't anything left to do until time to start dinner.

She went downstairs, reflecting that Paul had been busy. Less time at work gave him more time at home. She didn't even notice that her anger had dissipated while she did her few little chores and thought about her family. Nor did she realize that the intense emotions of the morning had exhausted her. She wandered through the sliding glass doors of the family room to the back yard. She seldom spent any time outdoors, leaving it to Paul to keep the lawn mowed and the few flowers weeded. She was a little surprised at how pleasant it was on this sunny autumn day.

Paul had planted a clump of tall snowball bushes in one corner of the fence and their leaves were bright red. There was a thin row of golden football mums in front of the snowballs, and the live fir they bought for a Christmas tree two years before was planted nearby. It made a pretty picture. A splash of lavender drew Elsa's attention and she went to look at a bed of fall-blooming crocuses; she didn't know what they were, just that they were pretty.

The kids' old swing set was still standing, albeit rather battered looking. She thought that in the spring they would have to get a baby seat so Sammy could swing, too. And a wading pool. They had thrown Paulie's away years ago or given it to someone, she didn't remember which.

But the kids had all loved to splash in the wading pool. The lawn furniture was still outside and Elsa sat in one of the chairs. It felt odd to just sit, with nothing demanding her time or attention, with no pressure to be doing something. She couldn't remember the last time she had had time for just sitting, enjoying the day.

It would be nice to have a deck out here, she thought. So they could use it even when the grass was wet. Maybe in the spring they could build one. There were stores she knew, where you could get plans and advice and all the lumber and so forth. It would be a good thing to have a place to gather the family in the summer and spend time together. Then her thoughts took another turn. She was out of work and Paul's paycheck wouldn't cover everything. Nor would their savings last forever. She'd have to get another job right away.

Elsa's stomach churned. She wondered how easy that was going to be, given the way her last job had terminated. But it wasn't her fault. Those anonymous letters were what had wrecked her and she had not the faintest idea who wrote them or why. Or why that reference to Zuzie and Paul had been on the back of one of them. Someone had written those letters to make trouble for her. Who? Why? Her mind oscillated between those two questions, but no answer, however tentative, presented itself. She had an enemy, that was obvious, but that was all that was obvious. She could think of no one who would bear her a grudge. It had to be someone who knew her fairly well, someone who knew her workplace and her family situation. That pointed to a co-worker but she could not think of any one of them who disliked her enough to do all that. She sat there until the sun dropped low in the sky and it started to get chilly.

Rhonda kept abreast of developments in Elsa's life by monitoring Zuzie's blog. When Zuzie wrote that her mother had lost her job, Rhonda went to work on the final phase of her revenge. It was so easy that it made her sick. So tragically easy. Several months earlier she had changed her electric service to a name she made up, Betty Sturdivant. She sent herself a couple of letters, addressed to Betty at her apartment address. She manufactured a social security card for Betty. It wasn't excellent but it wouldn't have to stand up to very rigorous inspection. Using those and a story about a house fire that destroyed her private papers in another state, she got Betty a driver's license. She took out a library card in Betty's name at a branch she didn't normally use.

One last piece of paper and she would be ready. This one was a little harder but not much. On the Monday before Thanksgiving she struck.

She put on gloves and a knitted cap that completely covered her hair and drove to a spot a few blocks from the daycare center, about halfway between it and the Mills' home. She timed it so she wouldn't be parked there long enough for people to notice her particularly. When she saw Fern coming, pushing Sammy in his stroller, she waited until they were nearly even with her car then stepped out in their path so Fern had to stop. Without a word she slapped Fern in the face, hard, then pushed her so she fell. While Fern was scrambling up, she jerked Sammy from the stroller and put him in the car. She jumped in and tore down the street with Fern running and screaming after her.

Rhonda drove to the office of Patricia Lester, a lawyer she'd been stringing along, although Ms. Lester thought she'd been doing the stringing. She was not too scrupulous, specializing in placing unwanted babies in adoptive homes. She was delighted with Sammy and handed Rhonda a manila envelope stuffed with cash. "Betty Sturdivant" cried at parting from the child she was unable to care for adequately, once again begged the lawyer to see that he was placed with loving parents, kissed him goodbye, and left.

Fern ran all the way home, sobbing hysterically. Paul was in the garage, painting his new bedroom. He heard Fern and ran out to her. She was pushing the stroller and he saw that it was empty. He caught her as she flung herself into his arms.

"Fern, what's happened? Where's Sammy?"

"The woman took him! Daddy, the woman took Sammy."

"What woman? Fern, honey, stop. Take a deep breath."

Fern screamed at him. "Sammy, Daddy! Sammy's been kidnapped."

Paul shook her lightly. "Fern, you're not making sense. Calm down and tell me what happened."

"Daddy! A woman jumped out of her car and snatched Sammy out of the stroller and drove away with him. Do something, Daddy!"

Paul's mind was blank. Do something. A child's faith that her father could always do something to fix whatever was wrong was amazing. Do something? The only thing to do was call the police. Then what? Call first and worry next.

Paul pushed the stroller into his room and closed the door. There might be fingerprints or something.

"Come in the house, Fern," he said.

He put his arm around her and led her into the kitchen. He helped her off with her coat and put her in a chair at the table. Her sobs were quieter now, and she watched Paul hopefully. He picked up the phone and pressed 911.

Chapter 19

As Elsa drove home from the grocery store, she was astonished to find the street in front of her house choked with cop cars. There were a couple of black sedans, one in the driveway beside Paul's van. She parked as close as she could and ran the rest of the way. Something dreadful had happened, that was obvious.

A uniformed city policeman stopped her as she was running across the lawn.

"Hold it," he said. "What's your business here?"

"I live here," Elsa cried. "What's wrong? What's going on?"

"Let me see some I.D.," the cop demanded.

Elsa hardly heard him. She tried to push past him but he grabbed her arm.

"I.D., ma'am. I can't let you go in there without seeing your I.D. first."

"I...it's in my purse. In the car."

"I'm afraid you'll have to get it."

"You don't understand." She was frantic.

"This is my house. I have to know what's wrong."

The cop guided her back to her car. "You don't understand, ma'am. I have to see your I.D. before I let you go inside. This your car?"

He opened the door and picked her purse up from the passenger seat. He handed it to her. She tore her gaze away from the house and looked at him. She took her wallet out of the purse and extracted her driver's license.

"See? It's me. Elsa Mills. Now let me go."

The cop compared her face with the photo on the license and nodded at her. "Go ahead, Ms. Mills. Sorry I had to stop you."

But Elsa didn't hear his apology, she was already running up the front steps. She went inside and stopped short at the family room threshold, bewildered by the number of police officials.

"Paul," she cried. "Paul!"

Paul was standing by the fireplace, talking to a couple of men in dark suits. Hearing Elsa, he glanced at each of them, then went to her.

"Paul, what's wrong? Why are all these cops here? What's happened?"

"Sammy's been kidnapped," Paul told her. "Come over here; I'm just telling the FBI about it again."

"Kidnapped." Elsa shook her head. "He's with Fern. She should be home with him any minute."

"Fern is here, Elsa," Paul said. "Sammy isn't."

Elsa shook her head again. "Where is she? Let me talk to her."

She saw Fern sitting by the card table. A woman wearing a dark suit was sitting across from her and a man in a dark suit was sitting with them. Fern looked distraught but in control of herself. Elsa hurried over to her.

"Fern, where is Sammy?"

"I don't know, Mom. He's been kidnapped and I don't know where the woman took him."

"No. No, he must be here somewhere. Were you playing out in the yard? Maybe he just wandered away. He can't have gotten too far. We'll find him if we all go looking."

The man at the card table stood up and faced Elsa. "Excuse me, ma'am. We're investigating. The quicker we get all the facts, the quicker we'll find the boy."

Elsa turned to Paul. "What's happening, Paul? Where is Sammy?"

Paul steered her to the couch and sat down with her. The two FBI agents he'd been talking to came over; one stood looking down at them, the other sat on the coffee table facing them.

"Mrs. Mills," the one on the coffee table began, "it appears that your son has been kidnapped. Your daughter says she was walking home from the daycare center, pushing the stroller with the baby in it, when a woman attacked her, knocked her down and grabbed the baby. She then sped off in her car. The girl can give no description of the woman or of her car."

Elsa was completely bewildered. "But that's absurd. Who would do that? Why? Things like that don't happen. People don't just grab children off the street."

The standing agent said, softly, "Yes, ma'am, they do. It happens with some frequency."

Elsa jumped to her feet. "Why are you all standing around here, asking questions? Why aren't you out looking for my baby?"

"Sit down, ma'am," said the standing agent. "We have to get all the facts we can."

Elsa looked around the room and sat down again.

"That's better," said the sitting agent. "We need to ask you some questions, Mrs. Mills."

"Me? Ask me questions? Why? I don't know anything about it. I just got home to find all of you here and my baby missing."

"Then that's what we'll find out. To begin with, where had you been?"

"At the store. The Safeway over on Stevens Avenue. We needed bread and milk, we always need bread and milk. And I wanted to get Sammy some teething biscuits..." She broke off and looked at her husband. "Paul?"

Paul took her hand and held it.

The agent continued his questions. "What time did you leave for the store? You went from this house?"

Elsa nodded. "Yes. I'm between jobs right now so I'm home most of the time. I left around two-thirty, I think. I don't know exactly. There was no reason to time it."

"What time did you leave the store?"

"I don't know. It's about a ten-minute drive. It took a couple of minutes to put the groceries in the car. What time did I get here? You must have noted the time. One of you."

"Yes, ma'am. Did you come directly home from the store?"

"Yes. I'd run some other errands this morning – the hardware store and the dry cleaners and I'd stopped for gas – what does all this have to do with getting Sammy back?"

"It's just routine, Mrs. Mills. We need to have a clear picture of everything around the baby."

"Mrs. Mills," asked the other agent, "if you are between jobs and were home all day, why was the baby at the daycare center?"

"I was looking for a job, I had calls to make and I might have to go on an interview at any time."

"How long have you been looking for another job?"

“A few days.”

“Why did you leave your last job?”

Elsa lost her temper suddenly. She snatched her hand away from Paul’s and darted across the room to Fern.

“Where is Sammy?” she screamed. “What did you do with my baby?”

Fern recoiled and burst into tears. Paul yanked Elsa back.

“Stop it!” he cried. “Stop it right now.”

Elsa turned on him. “Where’s Sammy? Where is he?”

“We don’t know, Elsa,” Paul told her. “No one knows where he is.”

Elsa shrieked at the FBI agents and the cops, “Find him! Go look for him! Stop wasting time here and go find him.” Sobbing loudly, she ran out the front door, only to be stopped by the police in the yard.

Paul knelt beside Fern and put his arms around her, whispering endearments. She was crying and shaking but gradually quieted.

“Daddy, oh, Daddy. I’m sorry. I’m so sorry.”

“Shhh. Honey, it wasn’t your fault. You didn’t do anything wrong.”

“Mom thinks I did.”

“No, she doesn’t. Not really. She’s just shocked and scared.”

The woman agent interrupted them. “Mr.

Mills, we'd like to see exactly where the attack took place. Fern, do you think you can show us?"

Fern looked from the agent to her father and back again. She nodded. "I think so. It was just down the street."

"Good. Let's go now before it gets dark."

The woman agent and her partner, with several crime scene investigators carrying their equipment bags, followed Fern and Paul outside.

Elsa saw them and tried to go with them.

One of the agents shook his head and told the cop beside her, "Mrs. Mills had better stay here. We don't want to compromise the crime scene."

"What does that mean?" demanded Elsa. "Fern is my daughter. If you're taking her anywhere, I should go with her."

"Her father is with her," the agent said.

"I'm her *mother*," Elsa insisted.

"Yes, ma'am," the agent answered. He spoke to the cop, "Keep her here."

The cop had to physically restrain her from following. Her fury began to give way to fear. They were treating her more like a perpetrator than a victim. Surely, they couldn't think she had anything to do with Sammy's disappearance. She must be imagining it. That would be monstrous. She shook the cop's hand off her arm and went into the house and up the stairs to her room where she paced around, trying to think coherently.

Fern led the agents and the cops down the street to where Rhonda had attacked her. There was nothing to see. Just a tree-lined suburban street of neat middle-class homes set in neat lawns.

"Was the woman already here when you got here?" the woman agent asked.

Fern frowned, trying to picture the scene. "I don't know. I think so but I'm not sure. There was no reason to pay any attention to the cars that were parked. Or the cars that were driving by, either."

The agent nodded. "I understand that, Fern, but it's very important to tell us everything you can."

"I know, but it happened so fast there just wasn't time to see much." Tears were rolling down the girl's face but she was making a valiant effort not to cry and to pay attention to the agent's questions.

"Tell us exactly what happened. Show us where you and Sammy were."

Fern walked a few steps forward and turned around. "We were facing this way, of course, going home. Sammy was in the stroller, strapped in. He didn't like to be strapped in but he sometimes tried to get out if he wasn't."

She looked around on all sides and moved back a few steps. "I was right about here. The woman jumped out of her car and slapped me. I was so surprised. I just stared at her. Then she gave me a push, really hard, and I fell down. Before I could get up, she had Sammy out of the stroller and put him in her car and drove away." She was sobbing then, and even the law enforcement officers were touched by her pain. Paul put his arms around her. When she was quiet again, he released her and the woman resumed her questions.

"What did the woman look like, Fern? Can you describe her at all?"

"Not really. It happened so fast. She was fat. And she had something on her head. A hat or scarf or something."

"How tall was she?"

"I don't know. Maybe not quite as tall as you."

"Did you see the color of her hair?"

"No, I told you, she had on a hat or something."

"How about her eyes. Do you remember what color her eyes were?"

"I didn't notice. I just had a glimpse of her face, you know, when she slapped me. After that I was on the sidewalk, trying to get up and stop her." Fern remembered something. "Her hands were blue. Dark blue. She was wearing gloves."

"Ah. That could be helpful. Can you remember what else she was wearing? A dress?

Pants? Coat?”

“I’m sorry. Just dark. I have an impression of her being dressed in something dark. I don’t think it was a dress. Pants and a coat maybe. It was pretty cold.”

Chapter 20

Rhonda waited a month, to let the cops and the FBI do whatever they thought they could do to find Sammy Mills. She continued to monitor Zuzie's blog and that kept her informed of the lack of progress in the case and of Elsa's increasing depression. She wasn't even looking for a new job anymore.

One Tuesday morning Rhonda decided it was time. She was excited and almost happy as she gathered her tools together for the interview. She attached a pen to her clipboard and put it in her big purse and made sure her questionnaire was also attached. She checked that her revolver was loaded and dropped it in the purse, as well. She also dropped a handful of cartridges in her jacket pocket, just in case.

She filled her tank with gas and drove to the Mills house. She drove past, looking to see if there was a car in the driveway. There was one but not two. She was sure that Paul and Elsa would each have a vehicle but had no idea if the blue Honda was Elsa's or Paul's. She was pretty sure that Elsa was home alone. Zuzie was still with her grandmother, Paul would be at work, and Fern and Paulie would be at school. If one of the children was home, it would only be a minor complication. She drove around the block, then parked at the curb in front of the house.

She went around to the back of the house, pulling on her blue gloves, thinking it would be better than using the front door with neighbors possibly watching. Sure enough, Elsa was sitting at a card table in the family room, playing solitaire. She was in a bathrobe and slippers and her hair wasn't even combed. Rhonda rapped on the sliding glass door and Elsa looked up, startled. Rhonda smiled at her through the glass. Elsa hesitated, then got up and opened the door a crack.

"Yes?" she asked.

Rhonda yanked the door wide and stepped inside, politely closing it after herself.

"What are you doing?" Elsa demanded. "You can't just barge in here like this."

"You know, I've always wondered why people say you can't do something you've just done. It seems so futile. But, then, you're a futile woman, aren't you? Come on, get your coat, we're leaving now."

"What are you talking about? I'm not going

anywhere with you."

Rhonda pulled her revolver out and pointed it at Elsa. "Oh, yes, you are. You have two seconds to get your coat."

Elsa hesitated and Rhonda slammed the revolver into her cheek. Rhonda was surprised how much she enjoyed it. Elsa staggered and only kept herself upright by clutching the back of a chair. One hand went to her bruised face.

"All right, the Ford's got a good heater, you won't really need a coat once we get in the car. Do it now because if I have to say it again, I'll shoot you."

Elsa let go of the chair and took a step toward the glass door.

"On second thought," Rhonda said, "we'll go out the front door. It's closer to the car. If your coat is on the way, you can put it on. But don't try anything heroic. All that will get you is dead."

Elsa snagged her coat from the hall closet as she passed it and preceded Rhonda out the front door. Rhonda put the revolver in her jacket pocket and kept it in her hand but she was pretty sure Elsa wasn't going to try anything. She was too shocked by the sudden invasion of her space and the unmerited violence. She got in the car and sat huddled against the door. Rhonda got in and started the engine. She pushed the button that would activate the child-proof locks.

"I never expected to use that button again," she said. "The one so the kids can't open the door. Since the kids are gone, I don't need it."

Rhonda pulled away from the curb quickly and drove sedately down the street, giving possible witnesses as little to notice and as little time to notice it as possible.

"You're the one, aren't you?" Elsa asked. "The one who kidnapped Sammy."

Rhonda glanced at her. "That's right. And if you behave yourself, I'll tell you where he is."

"Is he still alive?" Elsa barely breathed the question, fearing the answer.

"Oh, sure. He's fine. Sturdy little guy, isn't he? Cute, too."

"You monster!" Elsa lunged at Rhonda with her fingers curled into claws.

Rhonda fended her off with her right arm, using her left to steer to the curb as she braked to a stop. She managed to jerk the gun from her pocket and slammed it into Elsa's knee. Elsa gasped but kept trying to claw Rhonda's face so Rhonda smashed the gun into her face, breaking her nose. The pain and gush of blood stopped Elsa. She cowered back, whimpering, with her arms up to ward off any more blows to her face. But, much as Rhonda wanted to hurt her, physical violence wasn't her primary object. There was a scarf on the back seat and Rhonda reached back and got it. She handed it to Elsa.

"Here, use this."

Elsa took it mechanically and held it to her nose.

Rhonda put the gun back in her pocket and glanced around. They were still in the suburbs where people didn't walk much, in spite of the nice, wide sidewalks, and she didn't think anyone had been close enough to see what was going on in her car. She pulled out into the street and drove for some time in silence, out of town, toward the river. She turned in at a picnic ground that overlooked a wide bend where the water ran white over the rocks. There was no one else in the little park and the tables looked forlorn under the leafless poplars.

"Isn't this nice?" Rhonda asked. "My husband and I used to bring our kids here for picnics in the summer. Of course, you have to watch little ones pretty closely with those rapids right there. But I don't have to worry about them falling in anymore."

"What do you want from me?" Elsa asked. Her nose was swollen but had almost stopped bleeding. She was a sight with blood smeared all over her face and hands and caked on the front of her bathrobe. The bruise on her cheek was swollen and had begun to turn from red to purple. Her upper lip was swollen, too. Her whole face throbbed with pain.

"Okay, here's the deal. You are going to remain calm and in control of your emotions. You are not going to raise your voice. I'm going to ask you some questions. If you answer correctly, without getting emotional, I'll tell you where Sam is. Do you understand?"

"No. No, I don't understand at all. This is completely bizarre. You set me up in a situation that you know will stress me out of my mind and then demand that I don't show any emotion – you can't really expect that. That's insane."

"Ahh-ahh," chided Rhonda. "Your voice is going up."

"Of course it's going up," Elsa exclaimed, raising it even more. "You're asking the impossible."

"Ahh. Don't get emotional. If you think I don't mean what I say, let me assure you that I do. As for asking the impossible, that's what you asked of me and my husband when you took our children."

"When I took your children? I've never seen you in my life."

Rhonda gritted her teeth. "I know you don't remember me, I know I've put on some weight since you saw me, but you really should pay more attention to the people you ruin. It was all in a day's work to you, wasn't it? Just one more nuisance before you could go home to your own family. We were just riff-raff to you, people who didn't count, didn't matter. You thought we fit the profile so you took our kids away and destroyed us. Like stepping on a cockroach."

"What are you talking about? If you lost your kids, you must have been neglecting them or abusing them. You should thank me for protecting them since you wouldn't."

"Thank you?" Rhonda's rage boiled over and she had to pause to keep control of herself. "Thank you? My kids were not abused. They were not neglected. You didn't even investigate. You just took them away and I never saw them again. I don't know where they are or who they're with or if they're together or separated. All I know is, they're gone! And you want me to thank you. I want to kill you," she said. "I want to kill you so much. I'd love to hit you again and just keep on hitting you until you died."

Elsa flinched from the look in Rhonda's eyes and the tone of her voice, hatred concentrated and contained. Contained now but for how long?

"Do you remember taking a little boy named Griffin and a little girl named Logan because their stupid aunt told you that Logan had been molested by her father?"

Elsa nodded hesitantly.

"You do remember?" Rhonda insisted. "Don't

agree just because you think I want you to. The way you answer the questions I ask you is going to determine whether I tell you where Sam is."

"I don't know what you want me to say."

Rhonda smiled appreciatively. "I didn't know the right answers either. At the hearing. Remember? You had a clipboard and you asked us questions and checked the answers on your clipboard. And when it was over, our kids were gone. We knew in our hearts that we would never see them again but we kept hoping. We hoped that someone would investigate and find out that Logan's diaper was red from beets, not blood." Her voice shook with fury. "God damn you to hell! You didn't investigate. Your own procedural rules demand an investigation. You didn't even check to see if Virgil had any history of child molestation. You didn't even come to our house to see how we lived, how we took care of the kids."

"I can get your kids back for you. I can pull the files and show the judge that I made a mistake. I'll get them back for you, just tell me where Sammy is. Please, Paul and Fern and Paulie, we all miss him so much. And he must miss us. He needs his family. Please let us have him back."

"I wonder how many parents have asked you to give their children back and how many times you have just walked away from them. You could have held you hand, you could have given Griffie and Logan back to us. I wonder if you even took that diaper to the lab to have it analyzed. Did you even bother to read the report to know that it was beets?"

"I did," Elsa said eagerly. "I did, really. It's there in the files. All I have to do is pull it and go to the judge. You'll get your children back."

"You must think I'm a complete fool. No one can get my kids back for me now. I looked it all up, you know. I know that you people, you social workers, you people who think you know best about everything for everybody, you have decided that it is best to adopt out children as quickly as possible so their lives can be stabilized. I know that by now Logan and Griffin have been adopted. They probably have new first names as well as last name. I know that no judge is going to take them from a stable home and return them to a fat mother whose husband has left her, who lives in a crummy apartment, and has a janitor's job. So don't try to bullshit me. God, how I hate you."

"I was just doing my job. Someone has to protect the children. There are so many who are abused and neglected. You have no idea how horrible some people are to their kids. Someone has to step in and do the right thing."

"Stop sniveling. You were not just doing your job. It was never any part of your job to take kids from a good home with loving parents."

"But the facts. You fit the profile. I've seen so much of fathers abusing their daughters. The boy said he'd seen his father touch the baby's genitals. I did investigate."

"Virgil was a good father," Rhonda cried. "Good fathers change their babies' diapers. Can anyone change a messy diaper without touching the baby's genitals with baby wipes or a washcloth? I'm glad I did what I did to you."

Elsa reached up and touched her face.

"No, I don't mean just that. Although I'm glad I did that, too. I mean the whole ball of wax. I arranged for Zuzie to split and I arranged for Paul to lose his job and I arranged for you to lose yours. Then I arranged for you to lose your baby. It isn't enough to pay you back for what you did to me but it's something."

"You did all that? *You* did?"

Rhonda smiled complacently. "Oh, yes. I was behind it all. I'm not going to give you all the details but I wrote the messages on the walls of the boys' lavatory and I sent the emails accusing Paul of abusing Zuzie. I sent the anonymous letters that everyone thinks you sent, too. I did pretty well. You still have your home and your husband and two of your kids. But your husband sleeps in the garage – that should be you in the garage, by the way – he's completely innocent."

"You destroyed us. You ruined my whole family because I made one mistake. You're insane."

"I told you to stop sniveling. I couldn't possibly make you suffer as much as you've harmed me. I have nothing left. We lost the business and our home. My husband crawled into a bottle of booze and left me. This car is all I have left. I hope you are proud of how well you've done your job. Your former job. All right, enough of that. Now I'm going to ask you some questions. The way you answer them will determine whether I tell you where Sam is or not."

Rhonda took the clipboard and pen out of her purse.

"Don't worry about whether the answer is wrong or right, you have no way of knowing what the right answer is, just as we didn't know when you asked us the questions on your clipboard. But remember not to get emotional because if you do, you'll never get Sammy back. Here we go. Do you own or rent your home?"

Elsa closed her eyes and remained silent.

"Fine with me. It's no skin off my nose whether you get him back or not."

Rhonda started to put the clipboard back in her purse. Elsa opened her eyes and saw what the other woman was doing.

"No, wait, please, I'll answer. We...it's about

half paid for. Is that what you want? Money? We'll give it to you. We'll sign it over. Just give my son back to me."

"Elsa, you are dumber than dirt. This is not about money. Just answer the questions as I ask them. How long have you been married?"

"Eighteen years."

"Is this your only marriage, and Paul's?"

"Yes, for both of us."

"Do you have any other children?"

"Only Zuzie, Fern, Paulie, and Sammy."

"Pets?"

"We don't have any now."

"Have you ever had any?"

"We had a German shepherd once."

"What happened to it?"

"We had to take it to the pound."

"Why?"

"It was too big."

Rhonda made an emphatic checkmark.

"Do you ever yell at your husband?"

"Rarely."

"Does he ever yell at you?"

"No."

"Do you ever yell at your children?"

"Sometimes."

"Does your husband ever yell at your children?"

"Not often."

"Have you ever hit your children?"

"I have spanked them when they were younger."

"Are any of your children sexually active?"

"I'm not sure. Zuzie may be."

"Does she use birth control?"

"Yes."

"Elsa, you are so stupid. I put those birth control pills in her backpack. I knew you would jump to conclusions. Is that why she ran away from home? Because you didn't believe her?"

"She didn't run away; we just thought..."

Rhonda interrupted. "Don't make me keep repeating my threat. Answer the question and don't try to bullshit me."

"That might have been the reason. Part of it, anyway. She won't talk to me, just to her father."

"Have any of your children ever been arrested?"

"No, of course not."

"Do you take medications containing narcotics or other addictive substances?"

"Not usually. The doctor gave me some sleeping pills to help me through this thing with Sammy. I don't know what's in them. Please, tell me where he is. I can't stand much more of this."

"You just think you can't. But we're almost finished. Why did you leave your last job?"

"People in the office were getting anonymous

letters and they thought I was sending them. It was too much for me. I quit."

"I was kind of proud of those letters. Especially the one that had the line that pointed at you and looked accidental. But I have to give credit where credit is due, I couldn't have done it without you. If you had named your daughter Susie instead of Zuzie, I would have had to find some other way. But that unusual name made it easy."

Rhonda put the clipboard and pen in her purse and started up the car. She clicked the door locking button.

"You promised," said Elsa, nearly whispering.

Rhonda laughed. "So I did. But I only promised to tell you what I did with him. I didn't promise to get him back to you."

"Please. Give him back. I won't tell anyone about this. I'll make up some story about what happened to my face. I'll do anything you say, only give my baby back to me."

Rhonda reflected that Elsa was certainly a gruesome looking sight with tears wetting the dried blood and new blood seeping from her nose. She wished she'd thought to bring a camera. Her voice was harsh as she said, "I don't care who you tell. I don't give the smallest damn. I have nothing to live for. You took away everything I cared about. I took precautions not to get caught before today because I wanted to finish what I started with you. Now? Now I don't care what happens to me. So you sic the cops and the FBI on me if you want to."

"No, I won't. I swear I won't."

Rhonda eyed her. "No, I don't think you will. Because if you do, you'll have to tell them how you destroyed my family because I gave my baby beets for supper one night and you didn't bother to have it analyzed."

"I was having a baby," Elsa cried. "Sammy came early, before I got a chance to send the evidence to the lab."

"Don't start lying again. You had plenty of time. You just didn't think it was important. Did you ever remember those two little children you took? Did you ever bother to see what happened to them?"

"Yes. When I got back to the office after maternity leave. The lab report showed that the diaper had beets, not blood, in it. But no one could find you and your husband. You moved and there was no forwarding address. You abandoned your children so the judge let them be adopted."

Rhonda cried out and flinched as if she'd been struck. "Get out," she grated. "Get out of this car before I lose control and kill you."

Elsa opened the door. "Sammy?" she begged. "Where is Sammy?"

"I sold him. I sold him to a lawyer who sold him to a nice adoptive couple. He is happy and well taken care of and I doubt if he missed you for ten seconds. He may miss Fern, though. Now get out."

Rhonda gave her a shove and as she fell to the ground, drove away. The open door banged into a tree and slammed shut. Rhonda kept going and when she got back to the highway she turned toward the Interstate, away from the city.

About the Author

Barbara J. Olexer is a fourth-generation Oregonian. She has written more than twenty books and screenplays. Her first published book was *The Enslavement of the American Indian*, a nonfiction account of that little-known segment of American history.

Her formative years were spent in small farming towns and a backwoods logging camp. Barbara's life has been a tapestry of changes as she has lived and worked in small Oregon towns, such as Ashland, Camp Five (a logging camp that belonged to Kinzua Pine Mills), Klamath Falls, and Malin, as well as some of the country's biggest cities, such as San Francisco, Hollywood, Baltimore, and Washington, D.C.

On retirement, Barbara returned to the Pacific Northwest where her two grown sons and her grandchildren live. She lives in Milwaukie, Oregon, with her husband and two cats.